THE TERMINARCH WAR

Roger Colby

This is a work of fiction. Names, characters, places and incidents either are products of the author's imagination or are used fictitiously. Any resemblance to actual events or locales or persons, living or dead, is entirely coincidental.

The opinions in this manuscript are solely the opinions of the author and do not represent the opinions or thoughts of the publisher. The author has represented and warranted full ownership, and or legal right to publish all the material in this book.

This book may not be reproduced, transmitted or stored in whole or in part by any means, including graphic, electronic, or mechanical without the expressed written consent of the author except in the case of brief quotations embodied in critical articles and reviews.

For my kids, both in the classroom and at home.

Special thanks to my beta readers:
Jack Johnson
Jason Meuschke
Rita Colby
Carl Williams

Cover Art:
Jack Johnson
Twitter: @subjacktive

CHAPTER 1

Guillermo sat on a crate in the rusting heart of his decrepit cargo ship, contemplating the unforeseen waiting times that smuggling often required, a far cry from the glamorous adventures the holovids often promised.

He remembered watching one particular ancient Terran vid where a rough-and-tumble smuggler and his tall, hirsute side-kick had to float past a blockade of triangular enemy ships to fool them into thinking they were space garbage. He always thought the triangular shape of the ships was absurd, given the truth about faster than light travel. For example, the smuggler's ship would have been crushed like an egg. In actuality, smuggling (and for that matter, warp travel) was much less exciting.

Smuggling mostly involved sitting dead in space at out-of-the-way coordinates while a buyer or another smuggler made their way to the rendezvous. Guillermo usually passed this time by adding to his small pile of holo-files about the human female who had killed the bug queen and had subsequently ruined his life in other ways. He had managed to collect various threads of

1

evidence over the six months since leaving Dervish's home world. This was not a large number of files, mostly rumor and myths he had gleaned from various backwater dives and pirate space docks. He had several leads, all of them examples of the Terran woman's ability to cover her tracks with incredible precision.

When he wasn't dodging the bounty hunters who appeared at nearly every corner, he was trying to survive by feeding supplies and intelligence to the Ontoccans and their floundering resistance armies. This was not necessarily for the purpose of winning the war as much as it was for him to be a thorn in the side of the new queen of the bug home world and to eke out some kind of living. The Ontoccan Hegemony wasn't necessarily his ally, and some of the higher level leaders of their home world sometimes condescended to him, but he figured that the enemy of his enemy was his friend…or at least an acquaintance.

And above all, he needed to eat.

His fingers danced over the brushed metal table, mere centimeters above its grease-stained surface where a green tinted image of a star chart washed his face in an ambient glow. He flicked a control sensor and a few redacted documents and a curious looping clip of a shadowy figure entering a back door to the Skeev's club floated before him. The shadow actually looked more like a black spider crawling into a hole, but he swore it was the human woman even if Dervish had argued that it was just a trick of the light. The Terran woman had been masquerading as an Aldrassan aide to the former queen, and her holographic disguise was so convincing that Guillermo had not noticed even when she stood directly in front of him. He had been conned by her pretense of helping him adjust to being the last Terran in existence.

His pursuit of this side errand, and dividing his time between it and aiding and supplying the Ontoccan resistance, was the cause of a week long silence between himself and his blood-bound sidekick.

"Are you going to stare at those vids all day or are you going to help me inspect the cargo?" chittered Dervish, appearing in a paint-scratched doorway, leaning against the rounded frame. "I still think there are pests living among the crates. And if you'll put that fool's errand away for five micro-seconds we can get back to freeing my people from the thrall of the princess."

"Fool's errand," Guillermo said. "Sure."

Over three years cooped up with Dervish in this rattletrap of a ship had caused her to utter Terran speech with more of his mannerisms. Bug mimicry of human speech was usually measured, filtering through a set of five mandibles, their natural form of communication a series of body language cues and pheromones. At least they were on speaking terms again.

"Sure, Dervish," he continued, sweeping the images into a holographic envelope and closing it down. "I just wish I could get more information about her."

"You have been at this for over three seasonal cycles, Guillermo," she said, rubbing a jagged scar on her left cheek given to her by one of many bounty hunters. "I do not feel that we have gained much more knowledge than we had before you began this quest. It is not helping us end the war and is drawing your attention away from our mission."

"You mean theft?" laughed Guillermo. "We're pirates now, a far cry from the cop I used to be. Crulling shame. But you're right. Gotta press on with *your* fool's errand."

"It is not a fool's errand!" she hissed, her

mandibles twitching. "It is for the preservation of peace. The Queen is consumed by madness, and we must help the only group capable of ending her tyranny."

"It's a losing battle, Dervish," Guillermo replied, holding up a communique addressed to underworld boss Skeev from an unknown. "We should focus on the Terran woman. She's the key to all this...to the queen's death...the conspiracy against the Ontoccan Hegemony...all of it."

Dervish began to pace, the distinct pheromonal odor of agitation flooding Guillermo's nose.

"The queen has found a way to control her troops with uncanny precision, and some of the ships she has thrown at the Ontoccans lately have been new and unusual...much more effective than the re-fitted Terran hulks from ages past. She has also cut off the supply lines to the Ontoccans by gaining the support of the Guajiin. All the more reason to aide the Ontoccans."

"Exactly why we need to cut ties with them after this run, Dervish. Find the woman." Guillermo said, waiting for their speaking terms to become silence again. "We find her and the rest of this will shake out."

Dervish shuffled forward, her thin shadow

covering him, the odd perfume of her pheromones filling the room.

"We must continue," she said flatly, rubbing her scar again. "I desire peace, and the only way that will happen is for the queen to be deposed. I am unsure as to why my people have followed her so blindly. I fear we are not seeing the whole truth concerning her control over them."

"So you're saying she has mind control powers now? She's just lucky, that's all. The Terran woman connects everything, Dervish. I know it."

Dervish became very still, her mandibles growing slack for a moment, and then she continued.

"As usual you are acting without knowing all the facts. As I told you before, last time we encountered the queen's forces their scent was...wrong...as if they were sharing something between them. It is believed that in ancient times my people ruled the Five Rim worlds, but one queen saw the error in this, abolishing the terrible technology that allowed our hold on it for so long. I fear the queen may have unearthed that which was thought to be myth."

Guillermo smirked.

"That could have come in handy when the

Terrans arrived here. Why didn't they use it?"

"It is a thing of myth," she replied. "It is widely accepted that the technology was either destroyed or housed in some forgotten tomb. Most of my kind think it is a thing of fantasy."

"Well," Guillermo said, resting elbows on knees. "Looks like the queen has been doing some digging."

Dervish settled, seeming to ignore this comment. She instead reached past him to deactivate a warning signal for a power relay fizzling toward the end of its life.

"If we do not sell this shipment and pay back Ozdrack he will see to our demise. The true shame is being tied to such a criminal."

"Yeah," Guillermo offered. "The cycle of paying one criminal to get the goods to pay another one and then in turn using that to finance the Ontoccan resistance is tricky. But I live for punishment it seems. You can duck out any time you like, you know."

"I am bound to you, Guillermo," she said, nearly cutting him off. "You must not doubt me."

"Oh, I don't doubt you at all, Dervish. I haven't been the best partner, is all. We just differ on how to proceed."

"I am afraid that the Queen is winning the war," she said as she plopped into a nearby padded chair, her mind focused on one thing. "It is surprising that she has been able to unify my kind so quickly, even turning Junior and his band of pirates against us. Where do you think she is procuring this equipment?"

An alarm sounded and Guillermo rose from the lopsided crate, navigating by memory in the dim emergency lights as he darted toward the cockpit. Even though the ship was running silent, powered completely down except for passive scanning, something was approaching their position in haste and that made the hair on his arms stand up.

Dervish entered the cockpit just behind Guillermo to gaze through the plasteel window at a dark blob that grew in size, blotting out the blanket of sparkling stars that were sprinkled across the inky black of space. A faint amber light began to flash, nearly imperceptible to the eye but just within Guillermo's range of vision. It stuttered in the pattern of an old maritime form of communication still used by those who wanted to remain undetected.

A series of dots and dashes spelled out a message.

.-. . .- -.. -.-- / ..-. --- .-. / -.-. .- .-. --. --- / - .-. .-

-. ... ..-. . .-.

Ready for cargo transfer.

"Load it up," Guillermo said. "Looks like we're about to get paid. But Dervish, do your usual. Don't want to get too comfortable. Remember last time."

"Yes sir."

CHAPTER 2

After a series of maneuvers involving a complex dance of yaw and pitch thrusters, the yellowed and pock-marked hull of a battered old Terran cargo ship could be seen through the porthole outside the cargo hold. Guillermo aligned himself with the docking clamps of the other ship and when he heard the familiar metallic thud of contact he prepared the airlock for pressurization.

Dervish disappeared behind a stack of crates while Guillermo approached the airlock door. With a careful spin of a small wheel the door hissed open to reveal a pale-blue Guajiin, both sets of arms folded, tusked chin raised as if sniffing the stale cabin air for toxins.

"Hey there, big guy," Guillermo said, his lips slowly parting to reveal crooked teeth. "You're a little early, but as long as you pay up, right? You have the chids?"

The Guajiin unfolded his lower set of arms, reached behind him and produced a small satchel of leather that he tossed to the deck directly between himself and Guillermo. The grumpy giant then snorted, turned, and then disappeared into the darkness behind him.

Guillermo shuffled over, stooped to snatch up the

weighty satchel, then grabbed the handle of a nearby hover-loader and pushed it beneath the crates stacked neatly to his right. He flicked a control stud and it raised the crates off of the deck, allowing him to pull them along behind him with little effort as he followed the Guajiin into his ship. The connecting airlock tube needed work but it was sufficient. However when he entered the adjoining ship his sinuses burned with the stench of a race of beings whose culture forbade bathing.

Guajiins believed immersion in water actually washed away years of family tradition and heritage. Guajiin was a loathsome place to visit, and Guillermo had spent some forgettable time there, his only caveat to the journey a handy lexicon of alien profanity.

The other smuggler's ship was littered with the small bones of past meals and Guillermo was pretty sure that a stain in the corner was being used as a latrine. He tried to block it out, feeling as if he was breathing fumes directly from an ammonia bottle, but soon his eyes began to water. As he loaded cargo, the Guajiin would sometimes turn around to stare at him and Guillermo would smile, hoping that the big brute couldn't read Terran body language.

He was sure this Guajiin was not loyal to the regime
that had fallen in with the bugs, as his facial tattooing
revealed he was one of the outcasts of his world.
Guajiin settled all disputes…all disputes… with a duel.
Those who lost became part of the large group of
v'oshtu, politely and very loosely translated as "the
shamed". Shamed Guajiin made the best smugglers,
and if they were not working menial jobs on Guajiin
they were probably working for a crime lord, but never
as a lieutenant, always as a lackey.

The loading operation went quietly, the big Guajiin
not speaking. Not really helping either, but Guillermo
didn't mind. He was going to eat.

"Where do you want these last three?" Guillermo
asked, pushing the small stack of rectangular crates
along in front of him.

"Come," said the Guajiin, using a long fingernail to
dig at a bit of meat caught behind one tusk. "Stow
boom-sticks in lock safe. I display path to ship-belly."

Guillermo understood this to mean that the Guajiin
was showing him where he would be off-loading the
weapons. Guajiin brains had difficulty processing
Terran language, and a scarce few of them could utter it
without using strange slang terms, their own language

being made up of metaphorical descriptions referring to their own long and brutal ancestral histories. Guillermo was under the impression that the big guy wanted these last few crates stored somewhere that would avoid an inspection in case he was boarded.

Something in deep in Guillermo's mind told him to tread carefully. He had been betrayed before, and the massive revolver on the Guajiin's hip suddenly drew his undivided attention.

Reluctantly Guillermo pushed the crates along in front of him and followed the lumbering Guajiin down a series of musty hallways, all of them eerily quiet, the only sounds the heavy footfalls of the three-meter tall Guajiin and the soft hum of the repulser lift as it floated along. After a few turns down a grey, oil-stained hallway the Guajiin had pressed a large fleshy hand against a panel that opened a false wall, and they entered a second, slightly smaller cargo hold where several other crates had been stored. That was when the Guajiin turned to him and motioned with one of his thick arms.

"Here bed for boom-sticks, you," he grunted. "I give you meat, you load boom-sticks."

Guillermo turned away, thinking about the Guajiin

replacing the word "meat" for "money". An older slang term would be "bread". Without a word Guillermo scooted the crates into place and brushed a control stud on the handle of the load-lifter and pulled. As he did, he suddenly felt the markedly cold end of the Guajiin's gun barrel pressed against the side of his face.

The diameter of the barrel was as large as his left cheek.

CHAPTER 3

"Heap large payday scurry into snare," chuckled the Guajiin, his tiny nostrils flaring. "Bounty payday heap larger than cargo payday, but Auk'tor get all that chid, too, you."

Guillermo slowly raised his hands and then rolled his eyes to look at the Guajiin. The Terran stared calmly at the squinty black marbles that Auk'tor called eyes and wrinkled the bridge of his nose, his lips parting in a toothy grin.

"You have to be kidding me," said Guillermo. "I go to all this trouble to stay off the grid, try to help the only government with any kind of sense...a government that supports the liberation of your v'oshtu kind from your people's weird caste system, and this is the thanks I get?"

"Not privy, Terran. Not romance you, not red-face at you. Just payday."

"Yeah, yeah, nothing personal," Guillermo said with a laugh. "Well, this isn't either."

At that moment, a slender chitinous arm slid up and around the neck of the Guajiin and a narrow serrated blade caught the brute just under his thick jaw, slowly pressing through his gray flesh. A narrow line of blue blood dribbled down his neck. The huge gun dropped to the deck with a metallic thud and Guillermo put his hands on his hips and stared up at Auk'tor who was now being forced to his knees by Dervish's thin, razor sharp blade.

"Ooo, the nerve cluster," Guillermo chuckled. "For such a brute of a race, you Guajiin have some pretty lame weaknesses."

Auk'tor's many fingers twitched as he could only grimace and stare in hate at the Terran.

"I guess you probably know I'm the last of my kind," mused Guillermo as he casually sat on one of the crates and placed his hands on his knees. "Experiencing the death of your entire species is kind of sobering. It makes you think carefully about any business dealings, pretty much any relationship you have with others…as it may be your last."

Auk'tor tried to nod but only grunted when Dervish eased the tip of the knife into his skin. The hand that had held the gun was trembling, still outstretched. The narrow blue line of Guajiin blood grew a little fatter, dripping down and staining Auk'tor's ragged, greasy shirt.

"Oh don't respond…just listen," said Guillermo. He shifted on the crate, then stood and placed his hands behind his back and chuckled softly.

"There's this little j'umaa shop just east of downtown in Royal City…bug home world. You ever go there? Oh it's lovely this time of year. Not too humid. Just right for a hot cup of j'umaa. We Terrans used to have something called coffee, but the stuff the bugs make is pretty much the same, I guess. All the coffee died out because it wouldn't grow in the soil of any of the planets in the Five Rims. So the story goes. Such a shame."

Guillermo could see Dervish's legs wrap around the Guajiin's waist as she clung to him like a barnacle, her heels digging into his stomach. Guillermo brushed some dust from his jacket and continued.

"The death of coffee was a very sad day for the Terrans, I understand, as it was something they drank to shake off the grogginess in the morning. Had a high caffeine content…not as much as j'umaa…but I was told it tasted so much better. I so wish I could have tried some."

The Guajiin let out a slow breath, and Guillermo continued.

"There was a story about a Terran who tried to hoard away the last of the coffee, drinking a tiny espresso cup a week, but he was found out. Guy was killed for his coffee. Then another person from the the original hoarder's family died trying to steal it back. Eventually the last few coffee beans were lost right out a faulty airlock. Who knows? That coffee could be floating right outside our hull right now and we'd never know it."

Guillermo took three measured steps toward the Guajiin, eye-ball to onyx eye-ball, and then squinted, his jaw set firmly.

"I'm like that coffee, Auk'tor. Last of my kind. I'm rare, and I have survived all the other attempts to capture or kill me because I know how to sniff out traitors and pirates like you before you get the drop on me. Now if you agree to go back and tell the crulling v'oshtus who hired you that you couldn't find me, then delicate little Dervish here won't cut out an organ at a time until you finally die."

The Guajiin didn't make a sound, and Dervish tightened her grip like a constricting snake.

"Oh, I'm sorry," Guillermo laughed, patting the Guajiin on one trembling lower arm. "You can't really nod or anything. Just wiggle a finger if you agree."

One of Auk'tor's fat fingers twitched.

"Good," Guillermo said. "Dervish. Be so kind as to see Auk'tor here to one of his escape buoys, will you?"

Dervish slid from the Guajiin's back and with one flick of her hand popped out her electroglaive which extended to its full length. She immediately placed it at the back of Auk'tor's neck and gave him a shock that made him stumble forward, all four of his arms extended in a show of submission.

"You know," Guillermo added with a grin. "If you survive our encounter you could probably pop over to that restaurant on the bug world. It's really good... and I'm sure your kind is welcome there even though there's a war on. Nonetheless, you should probably tell your other bounty hunter buddies to stop trying to catch me or kill me or whatever. We've pretty much given them all the slip up to now and we're getting pretty good at it."

The Guajiin didn't respond at first, only snorted out a blast of snotty breath from his large nostrils.

"What of my boom-sticks?" Auk'tor growled.

Guillermo laughed again.

"Oh, I'm taking all of it and then I'm scuttling your ship after I strip it for parts, of course. Nice doing business with you."

"My clan brothers plant under dirt soon, you," mumbled Auk'tor.

Guillermo chuckled.

"Oh, I'm sure you'll try to get revenge some day. It's your Guajiin nature," he said. "However, I'll take my chances that you guys won't find me. Not to mention that other thug you call a boss. He's getting really desperate."

Auk'tor made an expression that passed for disgust, didn't voice it, and was led away silently. Guillermo began loading all the crates from the putrid smelling Guajiin cargo bay to his less putrid smelling cargo bay, wishing Auk'tor had made his move earlier so that he wouldn't have to load these stupid crates twice. He was happy to get free cargo, however, and a few upgrades.

A few hours later as Guillermo's ship vibrated, illuminated and then jumped through a spherical wormhole, Auk'tor floated along in an escape buoy designed for a Terran. His knees touched his chest and he screamed Guajiin curses into the small space that echoed and amplified his booming voice.

He screamed louder when he saw his stripped ship blow apart through the tiny porthole, the shockwave sending his little escape vessel hurtling away as if powered by thrusters. He closed his eyes so as not to be dizzied by the spinning field of stars, the centripetal force causing him to sink down in his tiny seat. He calmed himself, a slow process that involved some rather complex meditation and the invocation of ancestral names. With some effort he shifted his massive hand to run his pudgy fingers along one opposite wrist where a small band was located, and then he activated a switch.

Moments passed.

A blue light flickered and there before him projected in black and white on the interior hull was a dull grey helmeted figure, two triangular metal ears rising from the sides the mask like the horns of a demon, and a v-shaped slit in the angular face plate where two dark eyes peered through tinted plasteel.

Auk'tor summoned all of his courage but it was not enough to keep him from shuddering.

"Is it done?" queried an amplified voice, a combination of a growl and a hiss. Auk'tor could not see an expression beyond the hawk-like mask, could never see an expression.

"I am true bondsman," said Auk'tor, his deep voice ringing in the cramped pod. "Cargo loaded and sails furled. You track him like easy prey. I not so winning, though. I get payday?"

The helmet tilted slightly to the side as if weighing what was just said. Auk'tor could not hear anything, only the sound of his own breathing.

"Your services are appreciated, Auk'tor," came the raspy voice again. "You will find your compensation in the usual place. If you survive your current situation you can collect it. That is all."

"Can you not pluck me safe? In heap grand snare."

"Auk'tor," came the voice of the armored shadow. "I paid you to gain access to the Terran's ship and plant the tracker. Anything else is entirely at your own risk. It was all in the fine print of the contract. You Guajiin should start reading contracts instead of using your word as your bond."

The blue light of the projection winked out, leaving Auk'tor in near darkness save for the few lights that blinked on and off to indicate that the life support generator was functioning properly. He sat quietly for some time until his pod rotated around to allow him to see where he was going.

The yellow star of the Ontoccan system was usually beautiful to behold, its corona a lovely hue of red, but Auk'tor's scenic trajectory only caused him to scream.

CHAPTER 4

The fleet had been gathering near the dwarf star for some time, their black hulls new and glistening as they reflected the blue light, a product of years of planning deep under the cloak of subterfuge. The technology of ancient days was at last being freed from its tomb far below the once mighty city of the ancestors, and the queen mother would no longer be a hindrance to the plan to recover it, and rule the Five Rims as her people did eons ago.

Small fighters swarmed, each of them a narrow crescent with spines jutting from their hull like the talons of a predatory animal. They flew in and out of more massive vessels that held millions of bug shock troops, equipment and landing craft. Twenty dreadnaught class vessels hovered in the dim blue glow of the dwarf star, but in the center sat a massive control ship, a spherical colossus that had taken much of the effort of the bug race to build, created by the organic technology that had been awakened by the discovery of the unifier, the crown of subjugation, the C'Tuul'U'Hindra.

The Queen sat upon her chitinous throne and

twitched her thin fingers.

The throne had been built deep within a spire that jutted from the top, an observation deck that afforded her a view of the entire fleet. It was a fleet she had been preparing since long before the destruction of the Terran enclave on her home world, long before the lone Terran had foiled her plans.

It had taken her three long years to regroup. She had sacrificed the old Terran tech, the abominable traces of the invading devils, in a heavy bombardment of Ontoccan forces in orbit of the rebel planet. She had sent those ships, and their crew, to their deaths. She would rather lose them instead of the more powerful and ancient dreadnaught craft floating before her near this dwarf star.

She had been sending wave after wave, testing the Ontoccan resolve.

The destruction of her refurbished Terran fleet was only a setback. They were only meant to break through and find the chink in the armor of her enemy. She leaned back against her throne and wiggled her lower mandibles together, the left appendage severed by the teeth of the last Terran, but she would find him. She would have her revenge against him as well. She would eliminate the Ontoccan keystone, the thing that allowed them to uncover the workings of ancient Terran technology and spread them throughout the Five Rims.

She knew the nature of the keystone, the terrible secret the Ontoccans held, and vibrated with a seething rage that was alien to her but rippled down the tendrils of her new crown so that every drone nearby could feel the hot burning of her hatred.

She sat alone in her throne room, her long-sought-after prize sitting atop her almond-shaped head. It was the thing that had been buried long ago, centuries before the Terrans arrived, spoken of only in tales passed down by her royal line, and not favorably either. It had been the impetus for her people's voluntary technological atrophy that made them naive to the initial Terran invasion.

It was not a crown, for a bejeweled trinket was of little use to her.

The C'Tuul'U'Hindra was so much more.

Not long after she had returned from her pilgrimage to the outer swamps on her home world, a rite required of a princess, she had learned of an ancient ruin recently uncovered by a mining expedition.

To her people her newfound prize had become something of a myth, stories of how her people at one time were drunk with power, subjugating others and dominating worlds.

She had read the histories, the ancient stories of how her race was once a species to be feared. She had read of how they had built massive ships and explored the Five Rims, but that they looked deep into the heart of the universe and found something there that caused them to shudder, to fear the dark. Because of this they had taken on a monastic lifestyle, reverting back to the days before technology had ruined their sensibilities, a return to a more spiritual time.

She was told by her teachers to fear her people's past, to learn from it, but it only made her more curious.

During the last few years of her mother's rule, the princess had funded the secret excavation of the site with personal funds, covering the truth of her pet project with much publicized hunting excursions. Once her select mining crew had found the main chamber, a vast underground dome lined with hundreds of branching chambers, she arranged for the deaths of the entire crew to ensure its secrecy.

Sacrifices.

The next discovery was too fantastic to be believed, but it was real.

It began with a device, a small metallic rod with a curved end, which when held lit up the cave around her with a yellow glow, the handle somehow perfectly shaped to fit her insectoid hand. As she had held it aloft, it had crackled with a powerful energy that shot a bolt of yellow light toward what she thought was a solid wall, blasting a chunk of rock away, revealing yet another passage.

She explored deeper, finding a cache of weapons unseen by anyone for thousands of years, equipment that activated when her DNA was present, a treasure trove of a past unknown to anyone, buried deep within her own planet. She found a map of sorts to other things, other locations. Her memory recalled long forgotten childhood stories of the mistakes made by her race long ago, mistakes that made them shun this power. But she also knew that her people could be great again, that she could be great. She reasoned that if she could somehow harness this technology that they would no longer need the rusting, endlessly repaired tech left over from when the Phaedran Empire was ousted from the Five Rims.

She believed then, as she did now, sitting on her throne wearing the dread device long since thought buried, that the Five Rims could be rid of all influence of the Phaedran Empire, the wicked Terran filth that brutally ruled them for so long, enslaved them, and committed genocide against her own people.

She would set things right.

She reached up and ran her fingers along the edge of the C'Tuul'U'Hindra, a crown of chitin that spread its black tendrils up to the ceiling of her chambers like the limbs of a horrific tree. She felt the small barbs that clamped onto her flesh and burrowed in, a small price to pay to rid the Five Rims of all of the unclean.

She would make sacrifices. Had made sacrifices.

Her people would be free again, the Five Rims would be as it was before the Phaedran Empire, and she would restore her people to their former glory.

She could control it.

As she pondered this, dreaming of future conquests, Dlahuud the Aldrassan, the disguised Terran spy wearing an advanced holographic generator, immediately displayed a sweeping bow as she entered the chamber.

The Queen commanded Dlahuud to rise, using only body language as the mimicry of Terran speech disgusted her. The assistant did not need to be told what the Queen desired, and proceeded to offer information crucial to the Queen's plan. Dlahuud produced a data cylinder, a small pill-shaped device that she held aloft as she approached the throne. The Queen's black crown detached from tendrils embedded in the ceiling and folded down and across her back like black wings as she descended the throne to take the small device from her assistant.

Holding it before her she stroked a control stud and the Ontoccan battle formation floated in the air, represented in holographic diagrams and three dimensional models. She had a question, but otherwise would not have uttered a sound.

"Is this intelligence trustworthy?" she chittered.

"Yes, my Queen," said the spy, her true identity not known by anyone save Guillermo. "Are there any ill effects of the C'Tuul'U'Hindra?"

She shook her head to signify a negative response, but the spy knew the secret of the crown. The Divine Computat had explained its inevitable side effect, something that would assure their eventual dominance of this region once more, and then the universe.

The Queen recorded several hand motions and facial tics into the code cylinder, then handed it back to Dlahuud who then turned and carried it out of the Queen's throne room. The Queen ascended the stairs to her throne and reconnected with the millions of minds at her disposal, reconnecting to the hive consciousness that drove her armies forward. She watched through the immense plasteel windows as nearly a hundred newly reclaimed dreadnaughts opened a wormhole in space and jumped through on their way to Ontocca.

CHAPTER 5

As Guillermo's freighter emerged from the seemingly reflective orb of the wormhole, he was greeted with the view of thousands of tiny ships dotting the cosmos around him, flanking several dozen Terran-made cruisers and gunships waiting in orbit over Ontocca, a planet misshapen by the gargantuan Mount Coeius. Its colossal summit jutted nearly five hundred meters above the planet's upper atmosphere, its peak taking on the grey shade of a moon complete with craters and pock-marked near misses and a black crown of a Terran-made base at the top. The Ontoccan fleet faced away from the blue-green planet, their scopes scanning deep space for the onslaught of the next wave of bug battleships. After several increasingly difficult battles the Ontoccan forces were becoming weaker and more and more outnumbered.

Today, however, the sheer number of ships sitting in space was far beyond anything Guillermo had seen before. He noticed with absently that many of them were mere cargo freighters, outfitted with make-shift plasma cannons and patched-together armor plating.

The Ontoccans were pulling out all the stops.

Intelligence was shady as to how the Queen was producing starships so fast, how they were so coldly coordinated with each other when they attacked, and why they had been attacking at regular and decreasing intervals. First a standard month apart, then two weeks, and then one week. It had been three standard days since the last volley, and when Guillermo had emerged into real-space that day the small disposable Ontoccan fighters looked like t'okna hornets swarming out of a nest, but there were fewer than last time.

Something was up.

"Freighter *Terminarch* respond," squawked his comm system. "Proceed on heading mark, four six two by three two one by eight seven delta. We will load your goods once you dock, and thank you again for your service to the Ontoccan resistance."

"Pleasure is mine, control," Guillermo said, winking at Dervish who flipped some inertial compensators and dialed in the coordinates with nimble fingers. "Any word on the conflict?"

"We can talk more about it when you dock. Follow the flight line to the coordinates and we will see what we can do to provide maintenance to your ship."

"Too kind, control," Guillermo said. "But I don't

need any. A generous benefactor just donated most of his plasma conduits and hull plating before kindly detonating his power core. Such a kind chap, he was, too."

The dispatcher mumbled something about Terran humor and signed off. Guillermo conceded the controls to Dervish who expertly piloted the *Terminarch* along the planned trajectory toward a waiting battleship. The battleship began blinking its docking lights, a soft pulse of blue lines that guided the freighter in so the docking clamps could do their work. Moments later they stood in the cargo bay watching a couple of grubby Guajiin unload the crates Guillermo and his partner had so adeptly stolen. Each brute lumbered about, their leathery skin absent of the tribal tattoos of their race as they were not born on their home world.

Centuries ago the Terrans had brought large groups of every race in the Five Rims to Ontocca to mine precious ores and minerals, drain the oceans of sea life for foodstuffs, and to commit many other atrocities. The Guajiin, Aldrassans, bugs and Fraaz who had cohabited on Ontocca for over a century after the war ended were not connected with their cultures. Their individual ways of life had been ripped away, replaced by a clone of Terran ways, language and customs. For three centuries they had been slaves without cultural identity, but the century following the end of the rebellion had afforded them a time to create their own culture out of the ashes of the Phaedran Empire.

He remembered the Ontoccan motto: *As slaves we were unified. As free beings we will forever be so.*

Guillermo stood in the cargo bay, watching as the Ontoccans boarded his ship through the circular airlock. The two Guajiin unloading the cargo did not speak to him, but soon an Aldrassan, his slender legs helping him scurry along, approached Guillermo. The envoy, his hairless and almond-shaped head colored mottled red, nodded slightly in a half hearted bow, something left over from their lives as slaves.

"Guillermo March," said the Aldrassan, his Terran producing a slight lisp when spoken over rows of sharp teeth. "Your pay is waiting for you in your quarters on board our battleship. Please accept our apologies as we cannot allow you to leave as yet. I have been informed by the general that another wave of bug forces are on their way."

"Are you prepared?" Dervish asked. "The last battle was not as easily won as previous attempts by her royal crull-ness."

No reaction.

"We are confident that the supplies you have provided will be a welcome aid to our struggle," the Aldrassan replied, a single blink his only expression. "We have created a peaceful existence between the races here on Ontocca, one which we hope we can foster throughout the Five Rim worlds. The Queen's view that we are a threat due to our Terran hybrid culture is absurd. Her real reasons are hidden from us at present."

"I think I know what's up, Buraal," Guillermo offered. "The Terran woman we talked about before. She's key to this, I think. If we find her, I think we can probably get the answers we seek. She's gotta be behind all of this."

"Certainly, Guillermo," said Buraal, his eyelids flicking over large black irises. "I suppose that could be the answer, but there is more to this, I am afraid. She envies our ability to re-engineer old Terran technology. But the theory is conjecture at best. Right now we need to discover how the Queen is producing her ships on such a speedy time table. Perhaps your services could be used for espionage again? Your companion?"

Guillermo turned his head and looked at Dervish who was silently sidling up to him.

"I've told you before," Guillermo said. "I don't know what good it will do for me to return to the bug planet, or for Dervish either. They have bounty hunters after me, most specifically this Duuzra character. That *p'quuud* nearly had our skin if we hadn't limped into that nebula when he ambushed us last month. I'm doing everything I can to stay one step ahead of him, but he always manages to send one of his lackeys."

"I will volunteer for infiltrating the Queen's ranks," Dervish offered. "I am the most likely candidate."

"Chert no you aren't," Guillermo said, gently poking her shoulder with an extended finger. "I can't do without you, old girl."

"My people are being coerced somehow to follow the princess on this foolish crusade," said Dervish. "She is mad. Unfit to rule. I can mask my scent. I was born for this mission. It is the logical choice."

"Dervish," Guillermo replied. "Really, no."

"There is something ancient and familiar about the way she is waging this war, Guillermo. She has unearthed something from our past, I feel, something that was thought to be a fable…but we must discover the truth."

They all flinched as alarms began to sound and crew members scurried about. Guillermo saw two winged Fraaz fly past the intersection of the cargo bay's hall. Buraal tilted his head and placed a small hand against his tiny ear.

"The Queen's forces have arrived," he said. "Perhaps we should continue this discussion another time if we survive this."

"Yeah, yeah," said Guillermo, pushing the Aldrassan toward the airlock as the rest scurried along. "Everybody off! This ride's about to be mobile!"

The two Guajiin carried the last two crates out by hand as Buraal scurried out after them. Guillermo clumsily closed the door and then bolted for the cockpit.

"C'mon, Dervish! We don't have much time to break away before that swarm is raining down on us."

CHAPTER 6

Dervish wasted little time, following Guillermo the cockpit. They released the docking clamps, fired up the engines and felt the rumbling squall in the deck plating as they blasted away. Guillermo's eyes widened as he stared at the massive dreadnaught that emerged from the warp sphere in front of him. It was larger than most of the Ontoccan ships, which were simply rebuilt Terran battleships and fighters from the Phaedran Empire's occupation. This bug dreadnaught was something to behold. Its sleek lines like the shell of a giant mollusk were edged by spires that jutted from the bow like a bundle of javelins. Each sparkled with the violet light of its wormhole gravity generators powering down. Swarms of tiny crescent-shaped fighters began to pour from several ports around the outside of the dreadnaught, and the phase cannons all along its hull began to fire upon the old Terran battleships manned by the Ontoccans.

Buraal's ship took a direct hit, concussing its bow before they could raise the deflection array, and a large portion of the battleship's forward section emitted a cloud of atmosphere as it crushed inward, the pressure equalized by the vacuum of space. Debris began to plink off of Guillermo's hull as he dropped his sluggish freighter into a power dive, desperately seeking a hiding place within Ontocca's surrounding cloud of asteroids, but the old girl was torpid at best even with his jury-rigged modifications.

Seconds later he felt and heard the signature thump of disruptor blasts hammering his new ablative shielding. The scope flickered once, then failed, then blinked back on to reveal a quad of fighters on his tail followed by a larger craft that he didn't recognize, its wings spread like a giant bat.

Three flicks of his finger across the controls kicked in the afterburner and launched countermeasures in an attempt to fool the enemy's sensors, and he glanced back to see Dervish disappear down the gun well to man the rear-facing guns. Soon he could hear the comforting *thwop* of the proton accelerator as it superheated the carbon alloy that zoomed down the business end of the rail guns.

Two of the blips disappeared off the scope, but he didn't take time to fist pump the air, too busy cutting the inertial compensators back and holding onto his meager dinner. He rotated the stern 180 degrees to face his attackers, then punched the throttle hard to collide with three missiles that had launched only to listen to them bounce off of his hull before they could arm. One of the fighters trimmed its heading too sharp and nearly bounced off of the other, but now Guillermo could see the larger craft, lining up for a sickening game of chicken that caused the bile to rise in his throat.

On its bow, faintly seen in the flashing light of the plasma guns, the shape of a screaming Terran skull.

He rolled down and under the skull-ship's keel nearly scraping his starboard sensor array as he passed. The sensors sparked once and went out, and he banged them back to life with an angry fist, wishing he hadn't made so many cross-wired modifications.

A hiss of static erupted in the cockpit and then something broke through his comm line.

"I will capture you this time, Terran," came a raspy voice over the hacked comm. "It has been a challenge."

"Who the chert are you?" Guillermo shouted before clenching his teeth. He then held on to his seat as he slammed the freighter into a mad climb, Duuzra's hellish craft hot on his tail.

"Duuzra of the M'Hlaft clutch," came the voice again, its z's held a little too long, modulated as if from behind a vocabulator. "I will fetch a great price for you and the traitor."

Guillermo punched a few buttons on the comm,

unable to shut off the hideous breathing that filled the cockpit.

"Well, come and get me, you crulling v'oshtu. I got nothing better to do than to be the last hunt of your life."

An asteroid slammed into his port side. They were getting thicker now, as his plan was to hide in the remnants of an ancient moon that ringed Ontocca. He flew directly into the thickest cloud, looking for a large rock to fly behind and then power down like the last time he found himself in it this deep. He would have done just that if it were not for the limping Ontoccan vessel that was racing in ahead of him. It shuddered a bit, a strange vibration of the hull, and then it ripped open as its fuel cells failed and erupted in a blinding flash of blue-green light.

Asteroids began racing in his direction, pushed forward by the inertia of the energy burst. One of the larger stones bounced off of one the size of a city block and then crashed into a careening Ontoccan fighter, ripping the wings off of its port side before damaging the fuel cells, the small craft blowing apart in a million shards. Some of them bounced off of his cockpit window and caused him to grit his teeth, hoping that they wouldn't cause micro-cracks.

The alarms began to sound within the cockpit, a breach warning, starboard side. Before he could yell at her he saw Dervish crawl out of the gun well and dart out of the door.

He did his best to roll the ship beneath, at least from his perspective, a larger asteroid. He needed to get himself on the opposite side of that big rolling stone and get that bounty hunter off his tail. The oily scent of burning crystalline circuitry hit his flaring nostrils, his teeth gritting as he threw the freighter into a barrel roll that narrowly avoided a rogue boulder that would have embedded itself in his cockpit view-glass.

"Any word on that breach?" he shouted, but then realized he was speaking to himself. Dervish was incapable of hearing him, certainly unable to read his lips. He had to trust that she was hard at work trying to fix the problem.

Something astern echoed a metallic clang and more alarms sounded.

"The ionic coils are rupturing," said Dervish, appearing in the doorway of the cockpit. "We have to set down somewhere or we may rupture the power core."

"Crull it all!" Guillermo shouted, flipping a couple of jury-rigged failsafes and then sending the freighter into a power dive to avoid more asteroids that dwarfed his craft. His scanner flickered, but in the jagged lines of the grid he could see the unmistakable image of two bug fighters closing in behind him along with the bat-shaped, skull-faced personal ship of Duuzra.

He pounded the console with a fist of rage, then closed his eyes briefly, and reached out toward the wormhole generator control.

"What are you doing?" Dervish clicked as she watched Guillermo plot the solution into the FTL drive. "That is not advisable."

Without a word he fired up the gravitic emitters and punched the activation stud on the generator, programming in a solution to spit them out just at the edge of atmosphere. Their ship was then sucked into a reflective sphere forming before them. It looked like a giant magnifying glass centered on the planet Ontocca. Two screams later, they were spinning uncontrollably through Ontocca's atmosphere, hurtling toward Mount Coeus, its summit reaching far above the atmosphere of the planet.

He felt icy as the blood rushed from his brain,

Dervish pushing past him to take the controls, but she was unfortunately too late to make a difference.

CHAPTER 7

Guillermo's flicked his eyes open only to squeeze them closed again as the acrid black smoke filling the cockpit drove daggers into them. He tried not to breathe, but the need for oxygen forced his lungs open, only to have them pervaded again with the cough inducing fumes. No alarms sounded. The circuits operating those klaxons had apparently burned away in the crash. His freighter remained a heap of twisted durasteel, a scattered remnant of the junker Junior had reluctantly given him.

He tried to pull himself up, and that was when he noticed that he could not feel his legs. Something pinned him down. He struggled against it, his sturdy mechanical arm not much use as his rubberized fingers slipped and scraped at the chunk of paneling that held him fast to the deck plating.

Bright yellow flames burrowed inefficient tunnels of light through the smoke-shrouded cockpit. He looked around for Dervish, but only coughed a stream of saliva and then barely managed a grunt. In the haze he spied a long flat wrench and he was aversely thankful that his ship was so old that he had to repair daily. He grabbed at the wrench, fighting the urge to black out, his fingertips brushing it, nearly pushing it out of reach, then somehow he managed to grasp it and pull it quickly toward him. He hastily wedged it under the metal paneling and with all he could muster pushed upward. After a few painful tries he felt the paneling slide away.

His legs were completely numb.

Coughing, his lungs burning, he crawled along the corridor leading to the combination galley and nav-chart room only to find a jagged hole where the rest of his ship was supposed to be. He crawled forward, his mechanical arm sometimes hanging up on the exposed optical cables and power conduits. He cut himself on the shards of metal that protruded from the decking as he clambered out of the hole. After a brief moment of free-fall he found himself lying face up in a muddy puddle, the black smoke billowing out above him from what was left of his ship.

The cockpit had lodged itself in a very tall jungle tree, and he had fallen to the mud below, which had probably saved his life.

He still couldn't feel his legs.

He blinked his eyes, taking in the rich oxygen of

Ontocca, his lungs immediately expelling a gout of black mist as he coughed up the remainder of the smoke that filled them. He crawled through the mud, grabbing some nearby vines that dangled down from the massive tree.

The cockpit section far above him began to shift.

He saw it from the corner of his eye as he turned his head, but more than that he heard it. The howl of metal against tree bark, a high pitched grinding sound that grew louder as the immense chunk of his ship began to drop and then hang in the branches far above. Facing forward, digging into the mud with his arms, he pulled himself along, his lungs breathing in and out in a painful exercise, until he heard the final branch give way. He slogged forward through the slush as it finally crunched down in the mud behind him, a wave of brackish water pushing him along, its putrid stench flooding into his nostrils and mouth.

He lay in the muddy pool, time ticking by like the blur of stars in a wormhole, until he heard a soft organic clicking from far away, as if it had difficulty penetrating the thick wall of trees and vines.

Then he distinctly heard a roar that shook the ground.

"Chert," he muttered, and proceeded to frantically cover himself with mud and nearby underbrush.

The area where he had landed was a large clearing in the jungle, a huge scar in the foliage where his freighter had smashed through the canopy on its way down. Something blew the wind around the clearing like a hurricane as a hot beam of light shot out of the sky above, and his burning eyes followed it up to see the bat-like shape of the large gunship, the screaming skull carved into the metal of the bow.

Its angular hull, red with silvered scratches and dents, bristled with weapons and antennae. The triangular wings began to fold up as it descended, and the gravitic inducers caused little bits of rock and debris to float from the ground beneath it. It finally stopped, hovering just above the muck of the swamp, and a ramp dropped down from the mouth of the skull to reveal the crawling form of an enormous armored Fraaz.

He wore blood-red armor, pock marked with dents, scratches and burn marks. Guillermo lay in the mud, trying not to move, wondering where Dervish had gone to, and hoping that the bounty hunter couldn't see him.

"Do not try to run," echoed the amplified voice of

Duuzra. "It will only prolong the inevitable."

The predator's helmeted head, the faceplate a heavy v-shaped visor with an atmospheric mouthpiece that looked like the grin of a goblin, tilted to the side. The tall, directional antennae that rose from each side of the helmet twitched slightly, and Guillermo shuddered as Duuzra's wings unfolded, lifting the bounty hunter from the ramp to soar higher and higher. Guillermo lay still, listening to the sound of the massive wings, daring not to look above him, and then he heard a loud bang like someone hitting a taut metal cable with a heavy hammer.

Duuzra landed on top of his ship, one of the guns mounted on his shoulder thwipping out a cable that was hauling something toward the bounty hunter from the muck, a struggling form in a metallic net, the familiar shape of Dervish. She did not scream, only clicked annoyedly as his snare gun reeled her toward him, the cable disappearing into a slot on his armored back.

"Let her go, you *p'quuuð*!" Guillermo screamed, his arms pulling him forward. One of the crates of guns had shattered nearby and a few rifles lay in the mud.

"Wait your turn," Duuzra said calmly. "I will have plenty of net left to capture you, too."

Duuzra furled his wings and crawled like a spider down the side of the ship, some kind of magnetic grips in his claw-like boots and on his mechanically reinforced wings. The bounty hunter seemed unconcerned as Guillermo pulled himself feebly across the muddy ground, the peat strangely warm on his skin.

Guillermo's legs began to tingle.

Just as Duuzra pulled Dervish onto the ramp with a thump, a small rotating gun emerged from the armor on his other shoulder and shot her with a blast of compressed air and immediately Dervish lay still. The ground rumbled with a guttural growl as a long blue quadrupedal creature shot out of the jungle and pounced on Duuzra's ship. Casually and without alarm Duuzra turned to face the beast. The bounty hunter fired a mad volley of projectiles at it, orange tracers zipping into its gaping maw.

The lone creature slumped to the ground then, but this triggered a horrific retaliation from the creature's cadre.

A screech was heard that nearly deafened Guillermo and then three more swift-moving blue creatures emerged from the jungle, twice the size of the first, their heads somewhat reptilian, with forward-curling rams horns and a black spiny crest that ran down their twenty meter long bodies to the tip of their barbed tail.

Those tails flicked and swished, the barb a meter-long spike that dripped with a hissing fluid.

Guillermo willed himself onto all fours, his legs sluggish to respond even as the nanites in his bloodstream did their miraculous work. He slid in the mud once before stabilizing, then rose to his knees. The beasts ignored him, their claws scratching at the ship as Duuzra dragged Dervish up the ramp with him just missing the gnashing, razor sharp jaws of one of the creatures. Guillermo cried out, a raspy scream, nearly inaudible over the sudden roar of Duuzra's engines. All four creatures shrieked as they attempted to grab at the ship again, their teeth and claws scraping at the hull.

Duuzra's ship fired a few bolts of plasma at the creatures, and even though it pierced their thick blue skin they did not relent, leaping after it like dogs vying for scraps from their master's table. Guillermo watched in horror as his only friend was whisked away from him, and then held his breath as the creatures slowly dropped to all fours again, turning their arrow-shaped heads in his direction. Each beast blinked at him with two sets of onyx marble eyes.

He fell back into the mud, his mechanical arm held aloft as if to block a blow, and he felt them pad the ground slowly toward him, crouching low, their tails waving like pendulums. They soon towered over him, each at least six meters tall, and he noticed as a passing thought that each had a pair of small arms between their neck and their front legs, not vestigial, but folded up to protect nimble six-fingered hands.

He imagined that they would use these to rend the flesh from his bones in a more delicate manner than mere brutes were capable.

Their white bellies low to the ground, their bodies long and undulating, he could see sinews visible beneath blue skin, and jaws lined with rows of teeth like a cage made of daggers. He crawled backward, the nanites just now giving him feeling in his legs again, and he could feel the heat of their rank, animal breath as they approached.

Something shot over one of the beast's back and Guillermo was stabbed in the chest, then a cloak of darkness overtook him.

CHAPTER 8

Guillermo awoke, his head thumping.

He couldn't move. His arms and legs were held fast together by what he thought was some kind of blanket. He could move his head however, and he sensed that his hair was matted to his face, obscuring the vision in his right eye.

He was hanging upside down.

He struggled to move his robotic arm but could not, and as his eyes adjusted to the gloom he could see several other beings wrapped in some type of hardened crystalline substance and his nose was assaulted by a powerful odor of sulphur and rotting flesh. He stared at the multitude of faces, all from the various races of the Five Rims, all of them pasty white with death.

Each were wrapped in an ochre cocoon, hanging from the ceiling of a cave, the walls, ceiling and floors all coated with the same opaque crystalline material. He could breathe, but his arms and legs were completely immobile. He wondered why he was alive, and then he remembered the nanites, those little life-saving machines. Perhaps they had prevented the creature's poison sting from killing him.

He nonetheless felt very sick.

Lying all over the floor, silhouetted by the faint light filtering in from somewhere out of sight were several large ovoid objects, each of them covered with strands of the ochre material, and then he understood where fate had led him.

"Chert," he murmured. "I'm baby food."

The sound of his own voice echoed a bit and he could hear some rustling somewhere behind him. One of the blue-skinned creatures lumbered by and then turned to flare its nostrils at him briefly before scurrying away toward the light source behind him, weaving around the uneven rows of what had to be eggs.

Guillermo hung there silently for some time, wondering when these two-meter-tall eggs would hatch, wondering if he would starve to death before that happened or die from the blood pooling in his brain. He had a gruesome thought that the nanites might siphon off his bone marrow to feed his other cells, and wondered if he would become an emaciated husk of himself until he wasted away to nothing.

You can't make nothing from nothing.

Just then he heard another sound, a faint clicking,

and he stared in horror at one of the eggs a few dozen meters away from him, the top barely visible behind its counterparts. It began to shift back and forth violently. One of the beasts appeared suddenly, a blur of blue-black that skittered to the offending egg to nudge it with its snout, sniff around it, and then scurry away. The creatures monitoring this nursery were half as large as the ones that had spirited Guillermo away, but were still large enough to rip him to shreds with ease, each slender five-toed foot tipped with a shiny black claw as long as his forearm.

Another beast made a noise somewhere behind him and he braced for an additional sting, but it was a false alarm. His attention was drawn to the offending egg which twitched again and then broke open, a yellow-brown ooze pouring out onto the floor. He couldn't see what emerged, but he did see movement and shadows on the other eggs as something began to stalk toward him. He held his breath, waiting for his doom to emerge from behind one of the large eggs, and then he saw a bipedal humanoid dressed in slime-covered rags. It wore a woven basket of twigs fitted on its head, obscuring its features. It also carried a long spear, its jagged tip covered in gore and dripping with slime. It moved as if in a vacuum, producing no sound. Soon it stood just below him and he imagined that it was looking at him from behind that woven helmet-mask.

It grunted at him, poking the hard cocoon with its spear.

"I don't think that's a good idea," he whispered. "It'll just draw them in here."

An ancient saying, something about speaking the name of evil and it appearing, came to mind as one of the blue creatures scrambled into view, stopped, and then nudged the spear-toting intruder with its nose. The beast cooed and then darted away, and he heard what he thought was a laugh. A small laugh.

"What is the crulling deal?" he asked, still whispering. "Who are you?"

Without much ceremony, the being sliced the sinewy tendril that held him aloft and he fell, thumping to the floor and lodging himself between two of the eggs, which did not budge.

"Great," he said, this time aloud. "Drop me on my head. That will help. Good thing I'm wedged here or you'd have taken out the last of the Terran race. Great way to go out, I suppose. Fitting end."

"Shhhhhh!" hissed the figure as it crouched there in

the semi-darkness. With a few jabs of its handy spear
he fell out of the cocoon and managed to stand on
shaky legs. His rescuer grabbed him by the hand and
pulled him along, his feet dragging in the slimy mess.

They wove through the eggs and came to the broken
one, but there was nothing inside, only the nasty goo
his rescuer was wearing. His rescuer pointed with a
small five fingered hand at the broken egg and grunted
again, shaking its spear with the other hand. He took
the hint and then began to grab handfuls of the
lukewarm yellowed gunk and smear it on his arms and
legs. His rescuer dropped the spear to the ground only
to help him as Guillermo complied with the task of
bathing in goo.

He made the most unpleasant of faces.

Something was moving toward them, something
much bigger, and he turned to see a towering monster
lumbering toward them, this one twice the size of the
ones encountered in the jungle. Its forward curling
horns were covered with large spines, each as long as a
hover bike and its tapered jaw was filled with two
meter long teeth jutting in all directions. Its smaller
arms on the front of its chest reached out with long, six
fingered hands.

He felt a small gooey hand grab his again as he was pulled toward and under the beast. As they ran between the uneven rows of eggs he could feel it thunder above him, sniffing with dinner-table sized nostrils that sought out the intruders. They ran between its tree trunk legs and Guillermo had to duck as it swept its barbed tail over his head.

They ran, ran until they wheezed in the humid jungle air. Several beasts of varying sizes towered over to them only to sniff the air and then thunder away in confusion. The two escapees passed heaps of rotted carcasses, most of them the various fauna of this jungle, but some of humanoids of all Five Rims races. As they approached the edge of a clearing and pushed the underbrush aside to slide back into the jungle, Guillermo heard his rescuer utter what could only be a giggle. A soft high-pitched sound.

He opened his mouth to speak, but his rescuer darted into the foliage and he had to hastily follow.

After trekking for another kilometer or so, always wary of other beasts in the brood that might attack them, he followed the little humanoid as it scrambled onto a nearby low-hanging branch and then climbed the branches of a gargantuan tree, the limbs sometimes shrouded by hanging mosses. When they had reached a safe distance above the ground, high enough into the limbs of the enormous tree to see above the lower canopy where the beast's glittering nest lay in the distance, his rescuer pulled at the woven helmet.

Raven-black hair fell about his rescuer's shoulders and Guillermo stared at a beautiful olive-skinned Terran woman who gazed at him with narrowed, intense eyes.

CHAPTER 9

Dervish endeavored to sense her whereabouts, but where she was being held was dark and devoid of odors. The last she remembered was being captured by the bounty hunter and thrown in his strange prison, made from a technology she had never yet seen. At present, all around her was thick darkness, yet she knew she was being suspended from the ankles and her wrists were bound by some kind of organic fibers that squeezed ever tighter when she struggled. She felt like she was hanging in a vacuum, and the sensation of nothingness seemed to overwhelm her as dangled high in the air, the floor of this room somewhere far below in the darkness.

The room was suddenly washed in a yellow light, and after her optic nerves adjusted to the sudden change in lumens she could make out the shape of one of her own kind standing on the floor far below her. She could smell the unmistakable odor of the princess, now the Queen of her people, a traitor to the Queen Mother. She was flanked by two royal guards. Like Dervish they were bred for the specific purpose of being stronger, faster, more cunning, yet completely loyal to the Queen.

Dervish held no such loyalties for this upstart.

<At last> the princess twitched, using a combination of body language and pheromonal cues. <The traitor has come home.>

Unable to use body language adequately, Dervish exuded a scent that expressed a general opinion of disgust. The princess had betrayed her Queen, had assumed the throne aided by a Phaedran spy who was masquerading as Dlahuud, an Aldrassan aide. Absently Dervish wondered if the Queen knew the truth about Dlahuud.

<Save your response> the princess said, stepping closer to Dervish as she was lowered to the floor by what she could now see was a tangle of writhing vines and foliage. <My choker vine is very hungry. It has not dined for some time, and is in need of a fresh meal. You will tell me what I need to know, or I will make you comply anyway.>

<I will tell you nothing. You are a pretender to the throne, a spoiled underling who has forced her people to fight a selfish war. I am not thrall to you.>

The young Queen only moved near one of the writhing vines of the choker plant and stroked its thorny skin. Dervish could feel the vines tighten on her like durasteel cables that strained against her flesh and popped her joints.

<It is futile to resist.> intoned the Queen. *<In time you shall see the error of your actions. The support of this Terran should have ended when I assumed the throne. Your duty is to this crown, not to an outlander, a being descended from a virus that has plagued every system where they have resided. They conquer. It is what they do. It is genetically all they are capable of doing. Can you not see this?>*

Dervish relaxed, let the vines encircle her, wind their tendrils around her wrists and ankles, grip her waist with grinding pressure. They squeezed ever tighter, and she was thankful that she did not have Terran lungs for she knew that they would have burst by now. She angled her head at the Queen, and since she could no longer offer body language she simply spat acidic digestive juices in the Queen's direction and watched one of the guards become a blur to catch the fluid in her outstretched hand.

Dervish hung her head, her strength nearly gone. The Queen calmly opened her small hand to reveal two tiny mites that crawled up the vine toward Dervish, their bodies no bigger than a pinhead, their thread-like legs skittering forward to climb the vine higher and higher until they were poised beside Dervish's left eye.

Dervish croaked as they burrowed beneath her

flesh and deep within her brain.

CHAPTER 10

Guillermo had nearly given up speaking to this woman.

It wasn't that she couldn't speak, but it was like she only spoke when necessary, a product of living alone for so long he supposed. She would only nod now and again in agreement or shake her head for the opposite, and he wondered if her ability to speak had atrophied. Guillermo followed her willingly, knowing that he would be lost without her, and hoping that she indeed knew her way to safety. She motioned him on, and he followed her lead, climbing trees when she did and dropping to the jungle floor when she first scouted ahead and then beckoned him with hand signals. The predators who had captured him in order to feed their young were everywhere and their shrill vocalizations kept him awake at night. He did his best to sleep on the larger limbs high in the trees like his new companion. His lack of sleep was not necessarily because of the threat of the creatures, but because her snoring was something of legend.

She actually snored more than she spoke.

His mind spun with the thought that he was not

alone anymore, that somehow fate had brought him to this one place in this vast jungle only to meet another Terran who had somehow been dropped here, who had been surviving here for an unknown time. He had to figure out how she had ended up here, how she had survived.

He figured the mystery would begin unraveling with the act of learning her name.

As the morning light broke over the eastern side of Mount Coeius, he watched as she stirred and then made quick preparations to leave again. The dirty rags she wore clung to her slender body, and as he followed her he couldn't help but notice the slight curve of her ankle.

"Hey," he said, waving his hand around, ending with snapping his fingers centimeters before her small button nose.

She slapped his hand away and then snarled at him with her dark eyes.

"You have a name, right?" he asked. "I'm Guillermo March."

The corner of her mouth turned up and she blinked. She opened her mouth a bit, licked her upper lip, and uttered a soft "Hmmf."

"Yeah, not very spectacular, I know, but if you could just wait a second we could probably —"

"Mitsuki," she said, almost a whisper.

Before he could process what was said, she was gone, dropping down to the branch below and then looking back at him to wave him on, her face an impatient mask. He tried to respond but she was already climbing down the tree and he had to hurry to catch up.

They continued on their journey to wherever it was she was taking him, and often she would find insects and insist that he eat them. She would then promptly take to the trees again.

At mid-day they stopped near a tree with low hanging fruit, a tree that looked like a giant fern with leprosy - and smelled just as bad. He smiled at her when she held her hand up to her mouth, scooping the air and moving her mouth in a chewing motion, and he ate the fruit even if it smelled like it was competing with his horrible body odor. Surprisingly the fruit tasted better than it smelled, but not much better. What he could keep down kept him going.

After a couple of days they reached a tree much larger than any he had seen so far, closer still to the sloping face of Mount Coeius where the wind was a little stronger, and she began to climb it so quickly that he had trouble keeping up. His clothing was beginning strip to ragged remnants of cloth and as he climbed he tore his shirt so badly that it finally fell away from him and dropped to a lower branch. He found the tiny thorns of this new species of tree to be nearly unbearable. One scratch was fine and manageable, but not thousands, and over the course of several minutes of climbing he was beginning to become groggy.

Mitsuki looked back at him briefly, her eyes narrowing, her small mouth forming a smile, and she scurried down a few branches to take his hand. He waved her off, then her eyes widened and she shot her small hand past his head and pulled back a tiny reptile. It was long, slender and green. She held it aloft for a few seconds and then bit it just behind the neck. She casually tossed the reptile away, and Guillermo listened as it struck several branches on the way down.

"Poison," she murmured, and his eyes grew wide.

Mitsuki twisted her mouth, let out a sigh, and then pointed up, following her own unseen path higher into the tree where Guillermo could spy a platform far above him, a structure that was woven directly into three large branches. She scurried along, Guillermo following gingerly after, brushing aside thorns, and soon they entered a three by three meter hut just above the second canopy.

The wind here was stronger, and he could feel the tree swaying with the breeze, filtering in through open windows that could be covered during rainstorms using shutters fashioned from flat pieces of bark. The hut had spare amenities, mainly a low table, a stump for a chair, several free hanging nets that held various fruits and dried meats, along with a hole in the floor over in one corner, the purpose of which did not need to be mentioned.

"Home sweet home," said Guillermo with a chuckle, squatting on the floor and picking tiny thorns out of his arms. Mitsuki sidled up to him and helped him remove some of the pesky little barbs, but didn't help for long, her attention distracted away for a moment to shut the tree-bark shutters.

"How did you get here?" Guillermo asked, but she seemed to ignore him. "Like I said before, I'm Guillermo. I really appreciate you saving me from that nest. Really."

He paused.

"And you're Terran!" he said, doing his best to smile. "Our numbers are kind of few, you know."

"You talk too much," she said suddenly, her mouth turned down in disgust. "It was everything I could do to keep you quiet on the way here. Do you really want to be whiptail food?"

Silence save the sound of rustling leaves and creaking branches.

"You...you're suddenly pretty talkative," he stammered.

She leaned in close to him, as if he were a small child. Out of the corner of his eye she could see her small hand fingering a blade.

"I only speak when necessary. Whiptails are attracted to noise, not to mention scent. I only speak when I have something to say. You, apparently, haven't figured that out yet."

Mitsuki turned then, moving silently to one of the windows. She gazed out at the tops of the trees and the curving edge of Mount Coeius that rose high above them. She held up one finger, then slowly dropped her hand to her side, a gesture Guillermo did not quite understand. She crouched low then, creeping over to shut the crude door she had fashioned, dropping a board down in a groove that held it closed from the inside.

She looked at him and managed a faint smile.

He tried again.

"How did you know to get us out of that nest so easy," he said, the smile melting away. "...Or for that matter, how did you get in there...past the creatures? What's the deal? I mean, you — "

Mitsuki looked at him, her lips becoming thin, her eyes wild.

"Shhhh!"

He sat back on the floor, nonchalantly waved his robotic hand and stopped talking. She rubbed her nose, then moved in close to look at his metal hand, her small fingers tracing the rubber coated tip of his thumb. She audibly sniffed his hand, crab walked backward, then crept to the hole in the floor over in the corner and peered down to the branches below. She sat next to the hole then, rubbing her grimy hands together, humming a tune that Guillermo didn't recognize. He lay down on the floor, absently picking out the small barbs that remained in his flesh. Once he had pulled them all free he glanced back at her and noticed that she had slumped against the wall and fallen asleep.

He stretched out on the floor of woven branches and tried to do the same, but he couldn't. He couldn't stop thinking about Dervish and what was happening to her at the moment, whether she was being tortured or worse, and lamented the fact that he could do nothing about it at present.

His mind turned instead to Mitsuki, and as he watched her breathe deeply in slumber he marveled at the idea of finding yet another Terran like himself. She apparently was not from the place where the other Terran woman had gone. He didn't understand why she was here alone. He was tempted to wake her, to ask her why she lived here in the jungle alone, but he decided to let her sleep.

He knew that Terrans had been forced to live on the bug homeworld after the rebellion ended two centuries ago. Perhaps she was descended from a Terran group who defied the edicts placed on his people after the war. The Five Rims races had met at the Council of the Four and had voted to ensure that Terrans would never be allowed to be in control of anything ever again. The prevailing theory had been that genetically Terrans will turn to conquest and domination of others. The worst of the Terrans, the Phaedran loyalists, were sent off into the void in the world-ships they had originally used to reach this part of the galaxy. It was believed the ionic cloud had made short work of them.

Sure we're genetically prone to conquest, Guillermo thought. *That's why our remnant totally rose up and conquered the bug homeworld as soon as we could. We are so very dangerous.*

He stood up and approached a window, removed the piece of bark and peered outside. A dark shadow spread across the jungle, cast by the immensity of Mount Coeius, its summit reaching over five hundred meters above the stratosphere of the planet. Even though it was still daytime the light from Ontocca's star was blocked by the mountain's bulk, throwing the jungle into a strange blue twilight.

Mitsuki stirred behind him, suddenly rushing over to the window and yanking the bark from his hands, hastily replacing it across the opening and then securing it again. She hissed at him, then went to the opposite wall and climbed into one of the hammocks.

"Let's sleep now," she muttered, covering herself with a tattered blanket. "The whiptails will find us if you make too much noise. You can sleep in that over there. I'll sleep here."

Reluctantly he found the other hammock and after some difficulty managed to lay down in it. It nearly threw him to the floor a couple of times, but he managed to lay still enough to use it as a bed. He found it strangely comfortable, his body rocking back and forth with the almost imperceptible swaying of the little hut.

He stared across the room in the dim twilight at Mitsuki who began to snore again, and noticed that two strange words were stitched across the dirty blanket: "STRON" and "OLD". There was a significant space between the words, and it seemed as if they had been worn away with wear and tear. He thought he would ask Mitsuki about it later, then his eyes began to droop and he fell asleep.

He slept soundly, somehow managing to doze deeply enough to experience unpleasant dreams. After some horrifying monsters chased him a few times he felt pain along his forearm and knees as the hammock threw him to the floor again. The windows had been flung open, the daylight streaming through, and Mitsuki was suddenly offering him some dried meat and fruit.

He took it, ate heartily, and thought he would attempt to talk to her again between trying to chew on hunks of the strange meat.

"How did you get here?"

"I've always been here," she said, chewing a piece of that nasty fruit, her other hand holding an archaic book. Its pages were tattered and wrinkled with water damage.

She smiled at him, her lips hiding her teeth, and then she wrapped her tattered blanket around her shoulders and moved to one of the windows to peer out at the jungle. He knew that he had to get to a nearby Ontoccan base to find a ship...rescue Dervish...if she could be rescued.

He stood up and walked over to the window, listening to the branches creaking beneath his feet.

"I have to get to a base," he said to her, tapping her on the shoulder.

She flinched, then smiled at him again, squinted her eyes and then pointed out the window. He looked where she was pointing and could see in the distance the scar that his ship had left on the jungle. It wasn't terribly far from here, but not where he wanted to go.

"Ontoccan base," he said. "I have to get to an Ontoccan base. You know where one is?"

"I'll take you," she said. "When it's safe."

He walked across the floor and sat in the hammock, his eyes focused on the woven branches that formed crude planks under his feet. With a few playful bounds she stood by him, her hand pushing his chin up in order to raise his eyes to look at her. He stared at a face that was stern and solemn, with dark eyes that gazed at him intently.

"Base," she murmured. "I'll take you."

"Great," he said, a smirk passing across his face like a shadow. "When can we go there?"

"Soon," she replied, bit off a hunk of dried meat, and then went to stare out the window again.

CHAPTER 11

"So, are you leading me to the base?" Guillermo asked, gingerly pulling a strand of thorn-covered vine from his skin as he sucked air through his teeth in pain.

"The base is...well it's...this way."

Mitsuki only talked to him when she was sure the whiptails weren't prowling nearby, and when she did she told him that she had been living in the jungle alone for many years, that she had been abandoned by her father, but even those stories seemed convoluted and incoherent. He wondered if living in the jungle all of these years had driven her mad, but as they progressed she seemed to open up to him little by little.

They trundled along, now on the jungle floor, and Guillermo was amazed at how quickly the foliage and hanging vines caused his mind to lose all sense of direction. How she was leading him along was unknown, and that she knew where she was going seemed to him a miracle. She claimed that she was avoiding the "hunting trails" and for that he took her at her word.

He also noticed that they would stop periodically and she would look to the sky or to the sun-blotting image of Mount Coeius, the radiant light reflecting off of her olive skin. She said that the mountain told them that they were moving in a general direction of east or west, but didn't provide much more finite direction than that.

After some time, they emerged in a clearing, and there strewn across the ground were the remnants of his cargo ship.

"Crull it all, Mitsuki!" Guillermo exclaimed. "You brought me right back to the wreck. What the chert am I supposed to do with a broken ship?"

"Isn't this your base?" Mitsuki asked, her nose crinkling.

He reached out and took her hand and she pulled away from him and let out a small laugh.

"This is my busted-up ship!" he growled, very slowly, methodically. "I really need to get to a *base* where the Ontoccan defense force can help me find my *partner*...or get me off this rock."

"Rock?" she said with a smile. "This is my home."

Without another word, she walked across the clearing to the shredded cockpit section and began going through the damaged systems, pulling out pieces of metal and torn conduit.

"You can fix it, right?" she said, turning to look at him over her shoulder.

"Have you looked around?" he growled. "My ship is a compete loss."

He approached the wreckage, and after recognizing a couple of familiar components moved in beside her to begin tearing at a lower panel that hung agape. In a few minutes he was able to gather the parts he needed to build a way out of this. Apparently the communications core wasn't a total loss. He figured he could rig something to signal a nearby Ontoccan base and get himself rescued, to get them both rescued.

He crouched on the ground, fitting bits and pieces together, cannibalizing the power cell from a recycling compactor. He also pulled the high-gain transmitter from his fancy encoder and the circuit gel pack for the sub-processor that ran the atmospherics. He tapped on a few control studs and after firing it to life, powered it down, then fired it to life again and it finally gave him a reading across the encoder's repair screen that the scanner was operational. He sent out a few blips and beeps, a kind of spray-and-pray effort to get someone to notice his location.

He stood with his hands on his hips for a few

moments, his gaze focused on this feral woman as she tore through the worthless scrap and debris, and then he heard the distinctive sound of engines in the distance.

"Hey!" he shouted. "That was fast... You might want to get back to the tree-line just in case it's the enemy. C'mon!"

She turned, briefly glanced at the sky and then darted toward him, taking his hand and pulling him along through a painful bush filled with barbs. She seemed to ignore it, forcing her way through it, but he let out a frustrated scream at the familiar pain of the little thorns.

He really needed to find a shirt...or a suit of armor.

They crouched in the underbrush as a large, refitted Terran shuttle approached, its wings sweeping up on rotating hinges. The landing gear extended out as it blew swampy mist around the clearing and then squatted near Guillermo's wrecked cockpit section. Along the aft stabilizer fin he could see the unmistakable mark of the Ontoccan resistance force. He started to stand up, but Mitsuki poked his side with a remarkably strong index finger and he reluctantly decided to stay put.

"Not safe," she mumbled.

The landing ramp extended from the shuttle and three figures emerged: a heavily armored bug soldier and two Guajiin toughs, each carrying their giant revolvers. They immediately began searching through the rubble, pulling paneling aside as the bug soldier used a small hand-held device that looked like a life-form scanner.

"They are looking for me," Guillermo whispered. "C'mon, let's go make contact."

He tried to rise and she pulled at him again.

"Bad ones...hunters..." she whispered emphatically.

He finally fought her, however, pushing through the underbrush and then striding assertively toward the shuttle and the three rescuers. As he approached, the two Guajiin trained their revolvers on him. The bug turned around and then put his scanner away in a cloth pouch slung around his shoulder.

"Are you the Terran smuggler?" he chittered, his mandibles clicking together to form Terran speech. "We saw your craft go down from clear over at alpha base. Came to see if we could help."

Guillermo held his hands above his head and the two Guajiin did not drop their pistols.

"I wondered when you guys were going to get here," Guillermo said. "Too bad you couldn't rescue my partner before a bounty hunter made off with her."

The large Guajiin and the small bug gave each other a brief glance, one of the Guajiins nodded, and pistols were placed back in holsters. The Guajiin didn't move otherwise, and the bug soldier delicately skirted some rubble on his way to move closer to Guillermo. Guillermo glanced behind him toward Mitsuki but she was still hidden deep in the underbrush.

"Is there a way I could get a ship or a small wormhole-capable shuttle?" Guillermo asked. "I really would like to find my partner...maybe I could use yours?"

"All in good time," said the bug. "Right now we need to see to your injuries and get you to the base. So much to do."

The bug turned to the two Guajiin.

"Could you gentlemen see to Mr. March's passage back to base?"

One of the Guajiin rushed forward then, his four arms helping him lumber along the ground, and Guillermo staggered backward, tripping over a piece of twisted metal just before the bulky creature pounced on him and then held him down with all four arms.

"The Queen will reward us for this prize," said the bug soldier. "And then we will finally be rid of any trace of Terran culture."

"Chert," Guillermo mouthed as he squirmed in the grip of the Guajiin, the other one striding over confidently and producing a set of binder cuffs.

The Guajiin who had pinned him laughed a deep, guttural chortle, a string of drool falling across Guillermo's chest. He could feel his attacker's hot breath, the stink of a recently consumed raw meal. Guillermo looked into the beady eyes of his captor, but just then something was climbing up and over one muscular shoulder.

Mitsuki appeared, her gnashing teeth biting the stubby pointed ear of the giant. The Guajiin howled and reached for her with one of his meaty hands but in seconds a jagged metal spear head was protruding from his blue-skinned throat. Mitsuki twisted it into the back of her victim's neck, spilling blue Guajiin blood all over Guillermo.

The bug pulled out a disruptor pistol and aimed, but Guillermo twisted free and was rolling forward to gain footing, juking left just as the bolt hissed by him. The

other Guajiin fumbled for his pistol while Guillermo
rolled forward and knocked the bug to the ground.
The Terrran wrenched the weapon from the bug after
his knee crunched down on its upper thorax.
Guillermo then spun to vaporize the head of the other
Guajiin. As the headless Guajiin's upper set of hands
reflexively reached for a cauterized neck and then sank
to the ground, Guillermo spun in the other direction to
pistol-whip the bug across the eye, pulling back a string
of oozing fluid.

The muscular female stood atop her Guajiin victim
and grunted out something unintelligible, pointing a
blue-blood covered spear skyward. Guillermo spun to
see five bug landing craft approaching through the mist.
The ships dropped to the ground almost in unison, their
crescent shapes a new design that Guillermo did not
recognize, the hulls covered in a chitinous substance
that bristled with antennae and weapons like some
spiny giant wasp. The landing ramps dropped open
and rows of bug soldiers poured out, equipped with
plasma rifles, each of them moving in unison with the
others.

"More," she said. "They will bring more."
The two Terrans backed away, stumbling toward the

underbrush. However, out of the jungle a host of soldiers emerged: Guajiin, bugs and Aldrassans, wearing the signature black garb of the Ontoccan resistance. Swooping overhead were several armored Ontoccan Fraaz, their leathery wingspans casting shadows across the scarred ground, and that was when the energy bolts began to crackle through the air from every direction.

CHAPTER 12

"Run!" Guillermo screamed, blindly aiming at yet another descending bug ship and squeezing the trigger.

Three Ontoccan energy bolts sizzled across the clearing and cut divots in the hull of one of them, but it continued to descend, hit the ground with a metallic thunk and emitted a vapor as its inner atmosphere depressurized. A ramp quickly dropped down and a cluster of armored bug soldiers emerged. Dozens of Ontoccan resistance soldiers poured out of the jungle and into the clearing, their weapons blazing, seemingly ignoring the two Terrans running toward them.

Guillermo and Mitsuki were in the middle of a ground war.

Hastily, he stooped to pick up the components he had dropped on the ground, and Mitsuki grabbed his elbow at the same time. He dropped the gel-pack in the dirt and accidentally stepped on it, squirting greenish fluid into the weeds.

"Chert!" he shouted, a sizzling bolt flying just centimeters from his left cheek.

They were now nearly surrounded by the black uniformed cadre of Ontoccan defense force soldiers.

They represented all races of the Five Rims, their uniforms all the same onyx black armored unitard.

Guillermo looked for Mitsuki, but she was already on the run, and as he darted after her a Fraaz stirred the air around him as it swooped down, dropping an elongated bomb that bounced across the ground and detonated in front of a mass of bug soldiers. Fire and sizzling body parts flew in all directions. Guillermo, feeling the heat of the blast on his back, broke into a sprint and caught up to Mitsuki rather quickly, only to nearly run over her as she came to an abrupt halt. She spun around, her eyes wild with fear.

"Hunters!" she exclaimed. "Hunters have come!"

"Yeah, yeah! I get it! Look around you, sister!"

He tried to grab at her, tried to pull her along but Mitsuki adeptly pulled away, sprinting and weaving through the advancing Ontoccan soldiers, most of them bugs and Aldrassans. Guillermo turned to see the battle taking shape, many of the enemy bug soldiers moving behind rocks and debris from his own downed ship, some of them taking cover behind their drop-ships.

It wouldn't be long and they would be digging in. Guillermo spun back around and uttered a single syllable as Mitsuki disappeared into the underbrush. He staggered forward, attempting to move in the direction he had seen her go, but a huge Guajiin crouched in his way, close to the ground, firing his ancestral revolver at the enemy. When he saw Guillermo approach he waved him on, and reached out with one arm to hand the Terran a spare rifle.

"Hide in the tall greens, Terran!" the giant brute shouted. "Hold you in mother's arms!"

Guillermo understood that this was Guaji-slang for "you'll be safer in the trees" and decided to follow instructions, getting off a few choice shots at some straggler bugs who were trying to sneak around to a flanking position. He shot as he ran, his blue plasma bolts not very effective at all, and as he dove behind the slick trunk of a tree he saw the regimented and orderly ranks of the bugs filing off of their drop-ships. He felt a chill at their precision, all of them moving in concert as if under the control of one mind.

The Ontoccans were falling back, taking cover, and he could hear the leathery wings of several Fraaz swoop in from above. One of the Fraaz dropped near him, crashing through the jungle branches, getting tangled in the vines above Guillermo's head.

Something bounced nearby, a silver almond with a long rod protruding from the end.

A grenade.

He scrambled away just as it exploded, the trunk of the tree taking most of the blast and shrapnel. One small piece managed to burrow into his metallic shoulder. No pain, just an annoyance as he pulled the hot fragment free. More of the Fraaz fell from the sky then, dropping into the clearing like heavy strips of rubber, their cries silenced by some unknown sniper. Through the foliage he could see the glowing ends of several long-barreled rifles poking up from behind the wreckage of his ship.

"Surrender now and you will be treated fairly," came a familiar voice from the mass of bug soldiers taking cover behind their ships and the freighter wreckage. The voice, a strange vibrato, echoed off of the trees with the eerie volume of hundreds of voices speaking in unison. "Most of your forces have been routed and soon your world will fall to our might. We are C'Tuul. We are legion. We are one."

It was the princess. Somehow it was the voice of the princess. He recognized her particular double-clicking of consonants because he had injured her face last year, back when he was strapped to her torture table via her pet strangler vine. But how? She wouldn't risk her life here with the troops on the front lines. She was the supreme leader of the bug homeworld, surrounded by the best bodyguards, all of them like Dervish. Not even body guards could assure her safety in this war.

"We will give you a span of three minutes to respond," she said, her voice sounding loud, so loud it shook the ground, and that was when he noticed that it was coming from every bug soldier, all of them speaking her voice in unison, right down to her strange speech impediment. "After this time is expired, without your surrender, we will not allow you to live."

Guillermo peered around the trunk of the tree at the Ontoccans who stood just inside the foliage, their bodies swaying in hesitation. He looked past them to a section of bug warriors who were now emerging from behind one of the drop-ships. A dozen or so of them moved forward, their legs marching in unison as they stomped across the trampled grass.

"Witness our might," came their voices again, the unified voices of the new Queen. "Witness the might of the C'Tuul'U'Hindra!"

Guillermo didn't know what this "C'Tuul'U'Hindra"

was but he surmised that it somehow allowed the soldiers to move in unison and to speak with the queen's voice, to be controlled by her from some remote location. One of the Guajiin commanders, his black uniform bearing the gold insignia of his rank, shot his heavy fist in the air.

"Into the heart of death!" he screamed. "Brandish our weapons for dueling!"

At this command, plasma fire erupted from the forest, the blue glow reflected in the shiny green leaves of the foliage, and the small contingent of bug solders were instantly cut down. The shouts of several Ontoccan soldiers roared then, a small victory for them all, but it was drowned out by the heavy rumble of a ship overhead, a gargantuan battle cruiser that emerged from the heavy cloud cover, its hull still smoldering from re-entry, cannons bristling along its keel like the quills of a Guajiin sh'oktar.

The bugs would not be defeated.

Suddenly the forest exploded around them with energy blasts and Guillermo knew his only hope was to get to one of those ships. Get the chert out of there. He crouched low, sneaking forward through the clinging weeds, and then a hand gripped his metallic

forearm, and he turned to see Mitsuki again, her eyes
wide and frantic, tears forming lines in her dirty face.

"The hunters have come!" Mitsuki shouted, her eyes
wild. "Whiptail hunters have found our trail!"

As she uttered the last word, the blue-skinned,
horned beasts of nightmare began to rush into the
clearing from all sides, their tails thrashing and striking
at anything moving, their gnashing jaws biting their
prey in two. The heavy cruiser above opened fire on
them, and soon what was intended to be an organized
surrender turned into a free-for-all of chaos. The bug
soldiers scattered, many of them ran as if they had been
released from some kind of mind control and suddenly
realized they were in the middle of a war. In the air
hung the the pungent stink of pheromonal fear and the
acrid smoke of battle.

Guillermo hastily approached the Guajiin
commander who stood with tusked jaw gaping at the
spectacle, his gun hanging at his side.

"Now's your chance, sir!" Guillermo shouted above
the screech of one of the beasts, pointing at the
clearing. "Get your men to that drop-ship and let's get
back to base."

The Guajiin, his expression hardening, did not waste

words. He gave a signal with a wave of his hands and he and his few remaining forces charged around the outside edge of the clearing with Guillermo leading the way. Mitsuki trotted next to him, her spear bobbing. As they approached the landing ramp of the ship one of the creatures, a medium sized one, big as a hover car, turned its four blinking eyes on them and charged forward, a string of saliva dripping from its maw.

Mitsuki stopped, set her feet, then ran toward it.

CHAPTER 13

"No!" Guillermo screamed, his hand outstretched.

She ignored him, sprinting forward as the creature lowered its horned head and opened its jagged mouth, tail swinging around to strike. She leaped just as it came close, placed one foot on the edge of its forward curving horn and thrust her spear into its flesh, pole vaulting onto its spiny back. The creature shrieked, its tail barb shooting forward but missing, and she raised her spear only to bring it down with both hands and drive it deep through the creature's neck.

Guillermo wheezed out a string of Guajiin profanity and then continued to the drop-ship, disruptor fire scorching by his head as a few of the bug soldiers became interested in their approach. He didn't see Mitsuki's creature die, but he did feel the beast vibrate the ground as it fell noisily. Mitsuki somersaulted off of the creature's back and ran to them then, her spear covered in the black blood of the monster. She did not look at Guillermo, racing past him and up the landing ramp as the bug soldiers who had now noticed their approach moved in. The Ontoccan resistance returned fire as Guillermo ran up the ramp after Mitsuki. At the top of the ramp she was making short work of a bug who had left his post to repel boarders. After she had dispatched him, she darted further into the ship, leaving the dead bug slumped against the bulkhead wall.

Guillermo followed and quickly found the cockpit. There he surprised another bug with a front kick to the thorax. The bug coughed and slumped back in his chair. Pulling the soldier away and to the floor Guillermo fired up the engines, the controls somewhat similar to his own wrecked freighter, and the entire ship rocked as one of the larger creatures slammed against the hull outside.

The bugs had regrouped and were firing their weapons in concert at the predators, but their fervor had caused them to somehow forget about Guillermo and his Ontoccan resistance fighters. The Guajiin commander reached through the cockpit door and squeezed Guillermo's shoulder a little too hard.

"Distance between!" he said. "Wings up and dusting."

Guillermo let the throttle out and punched the inertial compensators as they lifted off the ground. As he peered out the cockpit window he noticed that the creatures were starting to retreat back into the jungle and that some of the other ships were lifting off as well, most definitely in pursuit. The big cruiser began to focus its guns on their little drop-ship.

"Does this crulling bucket have cannons?" he asked to no one in particular.

The Guajiin left him and he heard the commander's booming voice shouting orders at the remaining survivors. The Ontoccans, many of them ignoring their injuries, scrambled throughout the ship to find any outside gun battery. Soon Guillermo could hear the sound of plasma weapons and the unmistakable rocking and banging of the bug armada's return fire.

He banked the ship, the inertial compensators unable to keep up, and then shot out over the upper canopy toward the immensity of Mount Coeius. He had to find the nearest Ontoccan base and hope that they could provide reinforcements. He hoped the bugs were bluffing when they said they had conquered the planet. Out of the corner of his eye he could see Mitsuki's slender yet muscular frame as she adjusted her steps to the rocking of the ship and calmly sat next to him in the co-pilot's seat.

"So this is cool," she said, a near laugh, then touched the plasteel canopy with one grimy hand.

A flash of light in front of them exuded two beams that exploded inches from the canopy as the energy shields caught it, and he could see a bug fighter on a collision course with them. Guillermo dove down through the trees, spraying the air around the ship in a green shower of leaves, tree limbs being severed as they cut through the top of the jungle. Fighters zipped over them but then whipped around and closed in on their tail, but Guillermo felt like he was flying blind in this unfamiliar cockpit.

Guillermo's eyes flicked from what he thought was a scanner to the jungle canopy and then he gently adjusted the trim on the throttle.

"Gonna do something crazy," he said, his voice shaky. "Hold on!"

He heard one of the resistance fighters stumble into something aft, knocked some loose items about the ship. Guillermo pulled back on the throttle and funneled all energy output to the aft navigating thrusters, spinning the drop ship around and reversing its position. With a wince he dropped the ship down through a narrow clearing in the trees nearly scraping the wings as he rocketed down a giant sink-hole cave overgrown with vines. The ship easily cut through the foliage, but the blips on what could only be the scanner were replaced with warning flashes. The usual klaxons were instead flashing strobes because the bugs did not have use for sound.

He wished he had some sound.

Powering the maneuvering thrusters again he spun the ship around to drop down the hole backward so that he could see the entrance above them, a bright oval in the encroaching darkness. The wings of the craft at varied moments scraped the edges of the cave, but he managed to keep them facing vertical as the inertial compensators strained to keep the crew glued to the deck plating. The hole above became smaller and smaller as if descending down a massive elevator.

The Guajiin commander poked his large head into the cockpit.

"What be this magic?" he grunted.

Just then a blinking orb fell into the cave above them, dropped from a passing fighter, a move intended to end their struggle but a welcome move for Guillermo.

"Hold on," he said.

CHAPTER 14

Guillermo's metallic hand pressed hard on the console, shifting all remaining power to the forward shields. He heard something spark beneath the panel as the gravitic bomb exploded above them, sending chunks of rock and debris their way. This effectively shattered the energy shield even though he had routed everything including engine power. The ship dropped another seventy meters before lodging itself in the vertical cave with a screeching metallic crunch.

Guillermo was slammed back into his seat, the inertial compensators completely off-line, the entire ship's power off-line as well, and suddenly the air became very humid in the cockpit. He looked through the cracked plasteel above them at the light pouring in through the cave entrance, and he could see a pair of bug armada fighters floating down toward them to finish the job.

"Alright!" he shouted, stumbling out of his chair and dropping to the bulkhead door, one foot on each side of it. "Let's get the crull out of here!"

The Ontoccans didn't need further instruction. Their Guajiin leader barked orders to exit the landing ramp which was now facing toward the cave entrance far above them, an enemy determined to eradicate them descending fast. Mitsuki followed Guillermo, insisting on bringing her home-made spear, and he didn't say a word about it, reaching back to offer to pull her along even though she refused him with a wave of her hand and a curt smile.

They climbed out onto the skyward facing bow of the ship, and when Guillermo emerged behind them all he saw was the big Guajiin motioning him along with one of his four hands. They could hear the insipid whine of the bug fighter's engines above them growing louder.

"Terran," the Guajiin said, his head nodding as if he had a plan. "Safe in heart of the planet."

He was referring to a horizontal cave that was just meters above where the starboard side of the ship had wedged itself against the rock wall. They climbed along the narrow bow, stopping now and again to adjust their balance when the doomed craft would shift. Guillermo hoped that the ship would wait to complete its inevitable plunge to the bottom of the cave until after they had reached the horizontal passage.

Guillermo clawed his way to the cave, listening the increasing whine of the bug fighter's engines. They descended quickly, trying to stay aloft in the thick, damp air of the underground chamber. The crew of resistance fighters scrambled into the safety of the cave, turning to look behind them as the bug fighters began to fire upon their own drop-ship with blue-white plasma bolts which hammered it further down the pit. After a few well placed shots it finally gave way and dropped once again to inevitably explode somewhere out of view. The survivors sprinted into the darkness, the fire from the exploded ship only slightly illuminating their way as they journeyed further, venturing into the narrow cave where they hoped they could not be followed.

Guillermo was last to look back before trailing behind the group.

They marched forward, and after some time there was only the sound of dripping water and scurrying creatures in the darkness. The Guajiin flicked on a wrist mounted lamp to guide his way, and immediately some small creature skittered away from the light. The three-meter-tall commander shot one of his hands out toward Guillermo who managed to grab one thick finger and shake it.

"Commander Zuraal," he said, his throat rattling with the Guajiin's deep resonance. "I offer supplication for winner-duel."

"My pleasure," Guillermo said. "I guess. We were basically in the same situation, pal. Just trying to save my own skin really."

Zuraal pointed at Mitsuki.

"What of her?" he asked. "Be she your love mate, you?"

Guillermo laughed, and Mitsuki sidled up to him, mimicking his laughter.

"No way," she said. "There's this old Terran proverb...not if he was the last man on earth."

"Oh no," he said, giving her a sidelong glance. "She just...well she saved my life, actually."

Mitsuki placed a small hand on Guillermo's shoulder, her mouth a twisting smile.

"He's pretty useless."

The Guajiin stared at them both for a moment, a stern mask forming on his hard-chiseled face. A thought was forming, but Guillermo didn't really understand the expression.

"She good love mate for Terran," said Zuraal finally.

"Ha. Ha," Guillermo returned slowly. "Sure she is."

They walked along the winding cave. When they happened upon water they stopped to take a filtered drink and replenish their strength. The light from their wrist-lamps sliced through the darkness, mist filled beams shining as they walked steadily on. Guillermo noticed twenty or so variously injured soldiers, some of them worse off than others, and was thankful for the nanites coursing through his veins.

The only person comfortable in the darkness was Mitsuki, a person who had somehow saved him and now "tagged along." He couldn't help but be mildly attracted to her in spite of her insistence that he was the "last man on earth". Sometimes she would catch him looking her way and then she would offer that quietly wise and unsympathetic smirk.

He loved the smirk.

The strange circumstance of his meeting with Mitsuki weighed heavily on him. He didn't believe in fate, but somehow he was beginning to wonder if there was some order to the universe that led him to find the only other living Terran...other than the female who had royally crulled up his life and then disappeared into a wormhole.

After a while Zuraal trudged slowly beside Guillermo, his trunk-like legs much longer, requiring fewer strides. A long silence ensued before the Guajiin finally tried to make small talk in his own broken way.

"Not from this sphere, you?" he asked. "Where do you burn your home fire?"

Guillermo laughed.

"My *home fire* is on the bug homeworld, actually, I guess," Guillermo said. "But...doesn't word get around? I mean, I'm the last Terran...at least I thought I was. I had a bounty out on me, big guy."

Zuraal breathed out a puff of air from his mouth, a strange Guajiin gesture meaning a question was answered to satisfaction.

"Yes, yes...I have remember-drawn this about you, but your ancestry," he said quizzically. "It is March, your name of family. Do I walk true on the hunting trail?"

Guillermo stopped suddenly, the Guajiin turning to face him as the others passed by, their tired faces like blank masks in the gloom. Only Mitsuki looked back at them. There was that smirk again.

"Right," Guillermo said, his mouth remaining open. "March. Guillermo March. It's no secret who I am, pal."

"The maker of all has a plan, Terran," Zuraal said, turning to face a glowing light ahead of them. "Something brews in the stars. It is the maker who has aligned our lives together, you and I. You and the girl are the keystone. But I remember-drew you before that, before the bug world, and she before the jungle swallowed her."

Guillermo chuckled, placed a hand on Zuraal's large blue forearm.

"I don't believe any mystical mumbo jumbo," he said. "You saying you knew me and Mitsuki before we were on our respective planets? What do you mean? You know me from where?"

"Safe in mothers arms first," Zuraal said, moving on. "Keystone must be saved."

Zuraal lumbered ahead then, and Guillermo shrugged after him, a pained expression souring his dirty face. He always had to puzzle over Guajii-slang, but the word "keystone" he understood to mean something about the past, a way of unlocking a truth. However, Guillermo didn't have to think about it for long, as all of the others had now stopped just at the top of an incline where a soft glow lit the cave ahead of them.

"Up there," said Zuraal. "An opening leads to hearth of home."

Guillermo only nodded, his mind grasping at what Zuraal meant by calling he and Mitsuki the "keystone". Guajii-slang took time and effort to translate sometimes, but most times one could pull from it little nuggets of meaning.

Zuraal pressed his lips, blew a blast of air from his tiny nose and grunted.

"Home awaits," said Zuraal. "Gaze with own eyes, you."

Guillermo pushed ahead of everyone and climbed the tunnel, its slow incline rising to an opening where the big Guajiin waited. As Guillermo approached he could see the faint glow of lights that dimly illuminated a dome-shaped cavern. It was a large underground natural amphitheater. Several small plastic tents and portable buildings rose out of the haze.

A crowd approached, and they were soon greeted by a host of various Five Rims races, all of them wearing the signature black uniform of the Ontoccan resistance. They approached slowly, their clothing torn and ragged, weapons raised. Zuraal raised his upper arms in a display of peace.

The strangeness of the next few moments played out as Guillermo watched, all of the races of the Five Rims, once slaves on this planet, greeting each other as equals in a regimented military fashion, a hold-over from the days when their resistance movement was the first to rise up against the Phaedran Empire, against the Terrans. They had help, of course, from Guillermo's ancestors.

"Come close and hear the praises," Zuraal said, waving at Guillermo and Mitsuki. "Under tent of meeting we greet our family."

An Aldrassan male, his hairless body wrinkled and covered with mottled grey spots, hobbled forward using a long metal rod as a staff. When the band of resistance fighters noticed him they all bowed gently from the waist. Zuraal motioned for Guillermo to do the same, but he seemed to ignore him, placing his hands on his hips.

The old Aldrassan approached Guillermo and tilted his almond shaped head to the side.

"So this is the Terran male who has aided our cause for so long," he said, pulling at his ragged blue robe, smoothing it out. "It is my understanding that you fought valiantly before you crashed your ship."

Guillermo only stared at him, then looked back Mitsuki who was quietly winding a small strip of leather around the end of her spear where the blade met the staff.

"I guess," Guillermo said, turning back to the elder. "I appreciate all your people have done, really…but if it's not too much trouble I'd like to borrow a ship with FTL capability."

The Aldrassan cocked his head to the side.

"I don't know if that's…"

"Look," Guillermo said, his metallic finger pointing for emphasis. "I've helped Ontocca out more than I care to do actually. A friend of mine is in over her head right now and I need to go find her."

Silence fell on the group as Guillermo continued,

amazed that he was gushing out his heart to a group of strangers. In all the years of smuggling runs and near-death escapes he never realized that he cared so much for someone other than himself.

He didn't know how to proceed.

"I don't make friends easily…"

"You got that right," said Mitsuki suddenly, and he continued.

"And this…Dervish…she means a lot to me really and I just need to—"

"Our cause has gone to ground, my friend," said the Aldrassan, his slender hand reaching out to touch Guillermo's shoulder. "The grand experiment that was the Ontoccan alliance has crumbled from within. The Queen has taken all of our major cities and now we are trying to regroup our forces in these ancient resistance bases. I have hopes that we can unify again, as it was in my youth, but without vital supplies from the other Five Rim worlds I am afraid the fight will be long and brutal."

Guillermo listened to the Aldrassan talk about the rebellion and the plan to retake Ontocca, his face turning red, but then his focus landed on Zuraal. The Guajiin was not focused on the Aldrassan, but on Mitsuki, his mouth slack, looking like someone who was trying to remember a name or something he forgot. Zuraal's mouth pursed and his small black eyes squinted almost closed.

Mitsuki gave Zuraal a sidelong glance, then

approached Guillermo, touching him gently on the arm as the others listened intently to the old Aldrassan speak.

"Let's help them," she whispered. "We can leave here after that."

Her dark eyes scanned the group as she leaned in close to him, her lips near his ear.

"And after that…if they don't give you a ship…then I'll help you crulling *steal* one."

CHAPTER 15

The underground resistance camp consisted of neat rows of prefabricated buildings and some tents, most of them dented, rusty, repurposed storage units cleaned out and transformed into makeshift bunks, galleys, and a ramshackle, meager weapons locker. Guillermo and his faithful tag-along roamed the hazy camp freely after submitting to the understanding that they would meet with the commanders of the remnant in a few hours. Guillermo was informed that he was included in this group, and that it would take place after everyone had time to rest and lick their wounds.

The Ontoccan elder, who had finally introduced himself as Yalrykk, seemed interested in having two Terrans in his group, but the impression Guillermo felt from the elder was more sterile than welcoming. Centuries of slavery had conditioned their culture to exhibit a shrewd prejudice against Terrans subtly hidden behind smiles and niceties, and Yalrykk seemed to exude this smarmy attitude.

Mitsuki and Guillermo walked side-by-side toward the barracks, the musty odor of the cave pungent in the air.

Near the barracks three gunships were being retrofitted by a handful of Fraaz mechanics, blue bursts of welding arcs illuminating the underside of wings and open engine compartments. It was as if Mitsuki had seen an exposed silver vein.

"Should I go over and help?" she asked him, her dark eyes wide with excitement.

"Do you know anything about repairing gunships?"

"Nope," she said.

"You'll just get in the way, then," he said.

She frowned at him, an expression he decided he hated, and he looked away from it, noticing a few of the Fraaz mechanics taking notice of them long enough to mutter something to each other before returning to work.

"Do whatever you want," he laughed, like she needed his permission after all. "Maybe you'll learn something."

He watched a smile blossom then, and he decided that he wanted to see much more of that. She handed him her spear, and when she did her fingers lightly brushed his hand. In those few seconds he realized he had forgotten how soft female skin could be.

He watched her amble away from him, not telling her that she would probably want to clean up and get a hot meal, instead mesmerized by the way her slender arms moved when she walked. He waited there, wondering if she would turn over her shoulder and look back at him briefly, give him that smirk again.

She didn't

He sighed, then turned to walk a straight line to the barracks where he quickly enjoyed a brief shower and a hot meal. Afterward, he fell into a bunk and quickly drifted away to sleep. Yet in the darkness of his mind a dream began to play out.

He saw a small island surrounded by rough seas. The island was covered in a foggy haze and was also shrouded by perpetual night, and he felt as if he were moving closer, his disembodied mind flying across the choppy black waves. He soon flew between trees that towered above him, all of them slender and dead, with no foliage or greenery, only the withered bark covered with rotting fungus. As he settled to the ground, he could feel the ominous presence of something watching him, but he couldn't turn his head to see it. It was as if it were breathing on his neck, but the breath was cold and heavy like argon flowing across his skin. He stumbled forward, a small cave appearing in the distance, and out of fear he ran to it, but was soon surrounded by a group of Terrans dressed in white robes. One of them pulled him toward them. In his vision they all seemed taller than him.

He heard a voice speaking softly just out of range of being understood, mumbling something that sounded familiar yet still unintelligible. It sounded like one word, a word that all at once gave him hope but also filled him with dread, like a terrible trial that must be endured with the promise of prosperity at the end. The Terrans closed in on him, one of them offering an upturned hand, and in it a tiny ball of light began to form. He knew he had to reach for it, had to possess the light as it was something that he needed to in order to suffer through the trial.

But then something distracted him from the light — a scream. A rattling scream of a woman whose choked cries came from beyond a row of distant trees, a grotto where hazy blue light filtered out between wooden trunks like the fingers of a glowing hand. He pushed away from the Terrans, their arms grabbing at him. It was not to trap him, but it was as if he belonged to them, like a family, and he was running toward a horrible danger they could not stop him from chasing.

Something emerged from the glow in the forest, and he felt himself being picked up by a large arm, the ground racing along beneath him as he beheld two large legs pumping along, but he could not see who carried him. He could, however, look to his right past the hips of the runner to see another person being carried. It was a child, a small female child, her eyes and mouth somehow familiar.

And then he felt something press upon his face, and he opened his eyes to see Zuraal standing over him, his large tusks jutting from beneath his heavy lower lip.

"My nest is not yours," he grumbled. "Duel for your own nest."

Guillermo rolled over, placed his aching feet on the floor, and pushed away from the bed to stand on wobbly legs.

"Sorry, pal," he said, his voice hoarse. "Just kind of fell into this one."

The space now vacated, the two meter tall Guajiin sat on the bunk, its frame creaking beneath his bulk.

Watching Zuraal remove his sweat-stained shirt was a surreal sight as the upper two arms worked while the lower arms complied. As the tattered black uniform shirt peeled away, a cross hatching of scars was clearly visible on the Guajiin's wide gray back.

"You were a slave?" Guillermo asked, raising a querying eyebrow.

Zuraal's large head turned to look over one rounded shoulder.

"Time long before you. On the other side of the cloud. But you should know the telling of it, young one. Keystone revealed after rest of death."

Guillermo sat on an adjacent bunk, placed his hands on his knees.

"I thought that all of the Guajiin slaves had died out long ago given your people's average life span. I mean, you're no Aldrassan. And what do you mean 'I should know'?"

The Guajiin chuckled.

"Is this the way of your speech to the distant brother?" he said, his weathered face growing suddenly cold. "Know you not how to converse? Dark secrets hide in the belly of the beast. All will be revealed in time. The remembering scribe will come, reveal the keystone. Slumber now, I must."

Guillermo understood that the Guajiin had more to say about this, but the old fellow's eyes drooped and no Guajiin did anything without being fully rested. The Guajiin customs were thick with symbolism and strict codes of conduct, a flaw that allowed the Terrans to conquer their home world rather quickly when they first arrived in this region of space.

Guillermo opened his mouth to speak, to ask specifically about the "keystone", but Zuraal lay down on the bed, pulled the wadded blanket over his thick legs and rolled over on his side. Guillermo decided not to press it.

He started thinking about Dervish again, wondering what had happened to her, and then he started thinking about the gunships parked right outside...even if they were in bad shape.

Guillermo stood, dressed, and strode out the door of the barracks to find the old Aldrassan. It was time to con a ship out of him anyway.

CHAPTER 16

Guillermo emerged from the barracks with one purpose in mind: to borrow one of the gunships. If the old man wasn't going to give one up, then he had set his mind on stealing one.

As he strode toward the center of the camp, he glanced over at the gunships parked on a leveled off patch of cave floor, and he saw that Mitsuki was annoying a Fraaz mechanic who was trying his best to keep it together while she asked him question after question. Her arms were smeared with grease and she was chatting away at him, much more than she had done with him in the jungle, and he immediately began devising how he would use her in his con.

For now he let her do her thing, handing the Fraaz tools and cannibalized parts as he tolerated her high pitched voice. Fraaz had far superior hearing but poor eyesight, and the Fraaz had begun to flatten his ears against his head, a sign of painful annoyance.

Guillermo turned toward the center of camp, striding forward briskly, and through the mist could see the command structure, two pock-marked storage containers connected like siamese twins by a corridor.

He didn't get far, however.

"Where are you going?" asked Mitsuki who appeared at his elbow. He had not heard her approach at all.

"Getting off this rock," Guillermo said, striding

ahead of her. "Ontocca's a lost cause…none of my business. I've gotta find Dervish."

She caught up to him, her feet moving like a dancer, her hands black with grease.

"What's a Dervish?" she asked. "Sounds like a food."

"She's a friend," he said. "Look. I appreciate you getting me out of that pile of chert in the jungle but it's time for me to go find my friend. She's saved my crulling skin more than I can count, as I've done hers a few times, but I'm pretty sure we aren't even. If she even *thinks* I'm going to let her get ahead of me on that, she's got another thing coming."

Mitsuki uttered a strange exhaling wheeze. The snort at the end indicated that it was a laugh.

"Oh I have to go with you," she said, now jogging in reverse in front of him. "I'm pretty good in a fight. Can probably keep you from getting trapped again or whatever."

He considered this, but he didn't want to lose her, didn't want his bad choices getting her killed.

"Don't need you," he said.

She stopped in front of him, placed a small hand on his chest, and remarkably was able to stop him in his tracks. She looked at him with that irresistible smirk.

"I'm alone here. I realize that now," she said, her eyes narrowing. "I can't go back to that shack. I'm going wherever you go, even if I don't like you that much. We have to stay together, right?"

"Thanks for that vote of confidence, but there are worse things than whiptails where I'm going, believe it or not."

She stared at him then, her dark eyes scanning his face, then she stepped aside and walked slowly beside him.

"There are worse things than whiptails, even in the jungle here," she said. "But it looks like you and I are it...the last ones I mean. We should probably stick together is all. It would be a really bad thing if you died."

He laughed, strode past her, and then stopped when he noticed she wasn't following, and when he spun around her hands were forming fists at her sides.

"What?" he asked, arms out.

Her eyes flashed at him, then narrowed.

"I don't suppose you know anything about how I got to Ontocca...I have been here as long as I can remember. But I have these dreams..."

He took a step forward, hands on hips.

"What dreams?" he asked.

"An island, and then I'm carried by someone, someone really big...not Terran. There's a light that I need to guard or take or something. I don't know. I have them all the time."

His face became ashen, his mind whirling through the memory of his own similar dream. He didn't want to tell her, but he said everything with his eyes.

"You have the same dreams?" she asked. "What

does that mean? It can't be just a coincidence. I don't believe in them."

He turned, then looked over his shoulder as he strode away from her.

"I don't know what it means," he said, jogging now. "I'll have to figure it out on my own."

She followed anyway at a safe distance, and eventually he looked back again and she was gone. Somehow he knew she would be along on this journey with him, even if he wanted her to stay where it was safe. She had proven that she could hold her own in a fight, but this meant nothing. He wanted to ensure that his race would survive, and she didn't have the benefit of nanites coursing through her veins.

And he actually cared for her.

CHAPTER 17

The camp was beginning to bustle with activity, the Ontoccans emerging from their slumber to go about the difficult business of taking back their planet from the bug armies. Guillermo burned a straight line for command headquarters, which was a rather basic portable. When he stormed onto the front step, his fist rose up to pound on the door.

Boom-boom-boom.

He waited.

Nothing.

He pounded again, and something touched his shoulder gently.

"I told you I don't really want you alo—" he shouted, spinning around, surprised to see the wrinkled face of Yalrykk.

"These portable buildings are all we have, Terran," said the Aldrassan, his toothless pink gums visible. "You are early for the meeting, Terran."

Guillermo's face fell. He realized that he had one fist still raised to pound on the door and then dropped it to his side.

"Sorry, Yalrykk," Guillermo said, his eyes falling to

the cave floor. "I just needed to see if I could borrow one of those gunships over there and get on my way."

Yalrykk scratched his large ovoid head, the wrinkled skin mottled red and grey. His large opaque eyes reflected Guillermo's features somewhat imperfectly.

"I would love to accommodate you, Terran, and please call me Yalrykk. It is easier that way."

"Yalr—," Guillermo attempted. "How about just old man. Will that do? That name is a tough one."

"If you wish," he said. "Anyway, we do not have the resources to let you borrow a ship. We need all of them to assault Mine 4324. It seems to be the least defended of the bug spoils of war. I was going to ask for your help. You have, after all, impressed General Zuraal with your piloting skills."

Guillermo began to explain, about Dervish, about the life debt he owed her, about the bounty hunter, and how he desperately needed one of Yalrykk's broken down gunships.

Yalrykk listened carefully, covering his avocado shaped eyes with gray lids and taking in a breath through two tiny holes just above his small mouth. Guillermo could hear the noise of the morning around him, but he was focused now on the elderly Aldrassan who was attempting to calm himself before this impatient Terran.

He wasn't going to get what he wanted.

"All will be granted in time," said Yalrykk, his eyes slowly opening. "We are grateful to you for all you have done for us, Guillermo, and the desire of our heart is to help you with whatever you need, but my desires and yours are now outmatched by the current problem that is the bug occupation. We must strike now before they become deep rooted on our world, and more importantly we need to work our way to Ontocca City. Many resources are there, namely the old Terran tech…and there are things…things we need to secure there. Right now the Queen is forming her defensive shields, re-organizing her armies, and if we could just gain a small victory we are sure she might eventually be routed. Worse yet, she may have discovered our key to unlocking the Terran tech…all of our secrets."

"Yeah, but…"

Yalrykk placed a slender hand on Guillermo's shoulder.

"I was blessed by the God of all to lead the guerrilla armies that took down the cursed Phaedran Empire, your own kind, who ravaged the Five Rims for centuries. They enslaved and murdered my parents, yet we fought them and won with your ancestor's help. You are descended from the few Terrans who saw what their kind had wrought upon the races of the Five Rims, helping us stop the horrors of the Phaedran Empire. So please, I ask you, could you join me in prayer for your friend while we gain this crucial foothold? If we succeed I will not only give you a ship, but a strong crew to aid you in your journey."

Guillermo looked at the rocky cave floor.

"I'm not really a praying man...not really religious either."

"After all that you have experienced, you are still unable to accept that there is a power greater than yourself guiding you along?"

"Oh yeah," Guillermo said, his lip quivering slightly. "A higher power that stood by as my entire race was wiped out. I'm sure that's all in his master plan."

Yalrykk only tightened his mouth, his lips forming a thin line.

"Regardless," said the elder. "The meeting is in one hour. Our chief scout and tech expert, Jupriish, has subdued a number of whiptails with considerable cost to our resources. These beasts are crucial to our success and we would like you to use those piloting skills of yours to help us. My offer still stands. If you help us we will indeed help you. Your uncanny healing ability is valuable to us…more than you know."

"Yeah, I have that going for me."

The old Aldrassan bowed his head and clasped his six fingered hands before him, his voice muttering a faint prayer in his own language. He reached out a hand and touched Guillermo's forehead and drew an invisible unknown symbol there with a gnarled finger. Guillermo did not flinch, only closed his eyes in disbelief at the superstition of this elder.

Moments later Yalrykk turned, slowly striding away from him toward a crowded mess tent. The strange scent of alien food began to fill the air as Guillermo watched the old Aldrassan join the others. Each of them, of the various races of the Five Rims, greeted him with a bowed head and other body language demonstrating veneration. Guillermo watched quietly, then followed after them.

Later, as he sat at one of the open-air tables, quietly stirring a cup of j'umaa, he watched the battle-worn soldiers speaking to each other in Terran. All he could think about was Dervish.

CHAPTER 18

The strategy meeting was brief, and in Guillermo's opinion, it was a futile discussion of how they were going to attack a fortified city. Yalrykk was confident that they would catch the bugs in a transition between occupation and fortification, that they would be able to take out key areas before the bugs could rout their forces.

Much was discussed about the "secrets" in Ontocca City, that they needed to get to the tech facility before the bugs discovered it, but Guillermo noticed strange glances at him by Juuprish and Yalrykk, glances that made him feel more like an animal than a sentient being.

He chalked it up to that Ontoccan prejudice they tried so hard to hide.

The mine, however, was the first logical step to gaining a foothold for the eventual assault on Ontocca City, so it was agreed that they needed to take it out first. For a few moments Guillermo was sure that the Ontoccan alliance would fail the way they argued, but eventually they reached a consensus, and then all eyes fell on him.

A few hours and several repairs later, Guillermo dialed up the inertial dampers on their approach to Mine 4324. It took everything within him not to blast into orbit and leave them all behind. The mission seemed foolhardy, especially since his cargo hold contained the most uncontrollable variable.

His eyes blinked at the scanner.

A wave of fighters were approaching at full throttle.

His lone craft seemed even more solitary as he stared at the multiple blips on the screen. He flipped the switch on the automated plasma guns both fore and aft and then routed them through the targeting computer, his hands then firmly squeezing the yoke. Ship's power was drained considerably because of the plan and he ignored that first bead of sweat that rolled down his nose.

"This had better work," he muttered. "At least Mitsuki stayed back."

He considered his religious conversation with Yalrykk and uttered a softly spoken three word sentence to whatever higher power was listening. His heart told him that his words were lost in the void of space.

His craft began to vibrate violently as he pushed the throttle forward, zipping toward the host of bug fighters as if he planned to ram them. He could see them through the plasteel canopy now, oddly shaped black crescents with jagged spikes jutting forward. They were not of Terran design, something the bugs had built back on their home world and then shipped here inside their massive jump-ships. They were also very small, and he judged that only one pilot could fit inside their narrow fuselage.

But how did they build them so fast?

He plowed forward as the enemy began to form a hexagon, the ships in the center clustering closer and closer, nearly wingtip to wingtip, and Guillermo became very nervous that Yalrykk had placed too much faith in his ability to punch a hole through their defenses.

The comm crackled.

"We are on watch, Terran," came the gravelly voice of Zuraal. "You may strike at the heart of the prey."

Guillermo pushed the throttle as far forward as it would go, and he heard the first noise of his payload, a low growl echoing from reinforced cages in the hold behind him. That was when he felt a small hand touch his shoulder. He spun his head quickly to see Mitsuki standing near him, her other hand bracing against the door of the cockpit.

"Mitsuki!" he shouted, staring forward again, his eyes wide. "What the chert are you doing here? I told you to stay!"

She laughed and plopped down into the co-pilot's seat, fastening herself in.

"I couldn't let you do this alone," she said calmly. "You die, I die, remember?"

"You crazy w —"

He didn't get the rest of his sentence out as the first of several volleys of thread-thin yellow beams shot out of the swarm ahead of them, illuminating the modified shields on the bow like fireworks. The air outside the ship thumped with a crackling energy that shook their bones and shorted out several of the reconfigured control panels. One minor coupling spewed sparks all over Guillermo's left shoulder. He shouted, then boosted the gain on the shields hoping that what the old Fraaz mechanic swore to him would work was not a terrible lie instead.

Mitsuki laughed.

Guillermo only glanced at her with wild eyes, now sure she was insane.

"Hold on!" he screamed.

"Worry about yourself!" she shouted.

He could only watch in terror as the small fighters began to ricochet from his shields, sending sparks flying across his path. Many of them broke apart on impact but some of them remained intact, spinning out of control. He focused his flickering targeting computer on the mouth of Mine 4324 which appeared as a black dot on the shadowy side of Mount Coeius far ahead of him. He had to reach the entrance with his deadly cargo, a payload that was now screeching and roaring from the hold of his ship.

Juuprish assured him the stun collars would work.

"How did they capture so many?" Mitsuki shouted.

He ignored her, his hands flying over the control panel as he tried his best to keep the ship from flying apart. It only had to stay together long enough to get inside the mine.

He grit his teeth and then glanced at Mitsuki.

"You know how to release the loading door on the

cargo bay?" he shouted over the roar of engines.

"No," she said, her hands grasping at the arm rests of her chair as the entire ship bounced and rocked. The remaining fighters now fell in behind them and began a concentrated effort, firing on their unprotected aft hull.

"That switch right there!" he growled, hastily pointing at a flashing red light. "When we touch down, flip it!"

Seconds ticked by as the pounding on the aft hull became louder and more dire. Warning lights flashed, indicating that hull breaches were ripping open all over the ship. As they approached the ovoid entrance to Mine 4324 another wrinkle in the plan emerged.

Sitting just inside the entrance, mostly shadowed from the morning sun, sat a massive assault ship, its engines glowing in power-up mode. It was an old Terran model that had been retrofitted with some type of strange organic looking weaponry bristling from its forward hull. It was beginning to lift off from the tarmac, and Guillermo's ship was on a collision course with it.

Guillermo saw small spaces to the starboard and port sides of the assault ship crawling with bug soldiers, small specks of life that grew larger every second as his ship hurtled toward the opening. In response he cut in the reverse boosters but they responded only with a sputtering groan.

They didn't engage.

"Chert," he muttered.

The whine of the engines popped and died as the power core began to fail, and as he limped through the entrance and under the starboard wing of the assault ship, countless bug soldiers were vaporized by his overpowered forward shielding. The sparks from his hull showered the rest of the bay in a spray of molten yellow flame.

As they jerked to an abrupt stop, Mitsuki hit the button as instructed, but the power had been so drained that they didn't hear the cargo bay loading door drop. They would have to release it manually.

"How are you at getting past whiptails…especially really irritated and confined whiptails?" he asked as he released his restraints and grabbed a plasma gun.

She set her small mouth, her lips stretched in a tight line, then she followed him aft as a wave of hand held energy weapons began to pound the hull.

CHAPTER 19

Mitsuki and Guillermo reached the outer doors of the cargo hold, but the pounding and scratching on the other side of the door made Guillermo think the metal could probably buckle at any moment. The hallway just outside the cargo bay stretched from port to starboard and was lined with conduits that were leaking blue liquid coolant from new cracks in the seals. At each end of the hallway the airlock doors echoed from the plasma blasts of bug soldiers outside.

"What's the plan?" Mitsuki asked, her face somehow showing a glow of excitement. Perhaps it was the adrenaline.

"No idea," Guillermo said. "This ship is a brick, and the loading door on the other side of this cargo bay is not responding. We've got to get it open if we have any chance of causing enough of a diversion to get out of here. The Ontoccans are counting on us."

She rapped her knuckles on the door to the cargo bay. Something shrieked.

"What about this door?"

"You've got to be cherting me," he said, laughing nervously. "Remember all the whiptails on the other side? They're none too happy we just bounced them around with my stellar landing job."

"Is this the release for the door?"

He grabbed her wrist as she reached for it.

"No way! You really spent too much time in the

jungle if you think I'm going to just let them out...wait a minute!"

He ran over to the starboard airlock door and peered out the thick plasteel window, then reeled back as a plasma burst lit it up.

"There's a panel on the side of the ship...out there. If we can get to it we can manually release a pressure seal on the undercarriage. It would let the beasties out, but we'd have to run for our lives or we'd be eaten, too."

She jogged over to him.

"So we give up...or make them think we give up?" she said. "Sounds like a plan to me...a little crazy...but it might work. I'm in."

Of course. You like the crazy plan. It's bound to work.

He trotted back to the cockpit and grabbed two plasma rifles, then returned to the door and popped the safety on the manual release panel. The red light that usually signaled the alarm only glowed dimly in protest.

"You ready?" he asked.

She didn't respond, only grabbed a plasma rifle from his hand and after some fumbling flipped the power selector, producing a high pitched whine as it cycled its relays.

He pulled the lever down and the door cracked open, a hiss of depressurized air escaping and causing their ears to pop. A plasma bolt sizzled into the hallway and past them, rupturing a control panel, its only response a weak shower of sparks.

"We give up!" Guillermo shouted, sticking his plasma rifle out the crack in the door, its bulk hanging by the strap in his hand.

She stared at him, her face a blank stare.

He rolled his eyes, remembering that bugs couldn't hear him and couldn't read his lips, so he dropped the gun out of the crack and listened to it clatter to the tarmac.

"They'll get it," he said, offering Mitsuki a worn smile.

She offered a smirk.

Through the crack between the thick sliding doors he could see the crowd of bug soldiers backing away, their guns raised. A green skinned military command bug parted their numbers as he moved to the front of their ranks. He held a small plasma pistol which he kept trained on the door. His five sets of mandibles began to click together in the approximation of Terran speech.

"It is sickening to have to speak your cursed language, Terran," he said, his almond shaped head twitching in a body language display of disgust. "Throw your other weapons out onto the tarmac and we shall discuss the terms of your surrender."

Mitsuki shrugged and then tossed her rifle out onto the tarmac. The ship in ruins, the two Terrans stared at each other, gaining strength from each other, each of them building the courage to do what came next.

As two bug soldiers removed the weapons from the

tarmac, two grimy hands appeared in the crack between the doors, forced them open with a grunt, and Guillermo emerged, followed closely by a grinning Mitsuki. The Terrans raised their hands awkwardly above their heads and their eyes blinked as they adjusted to the morning light. They stood on the threshold lip of the airlock just above the tarmac, like standing on the running board of a hover truck, and Guillermo's eyes flicked to his left to see the manual lever that controlled the cargo bay emergency purge hatch.

It was inches away.

He cleared his throat.

"We don't want to die, that's sure," Guillermo said. "Just give us a sec —"

"You will descend from that hatch and get to your knees!" hissed the command bug. "Then we shall take you to the Queen. Her majesty will be pleased with us that we caught her greatest enemy...and that we also found another Terran for her to exterminate."

"Yeah, that's all well and good...glad for you, pal. Just let me get d —"

Guillermo dropped to the tarmac, but then rolled to his left into the waiting clawed hands of three bug soldiers. Mitsuki leaped from the airlock door, clearing the ground, and planted both feet directly into the thorax of the bug commander, crushing him to the ground. Plasma bolts sizzled the air around them as Guillermo fought through the bug soldiers, his mechanical fist pounding them aside. He dropped three of them rather quickly and as he grabbed a fourth by the throat, hoisting the soldier to the hull of his ship and pinning him there with a clang, he saw that the release lever was a few steps away. Wading through them he was able to pull down on the emergency hatch, then the explosives in the seams of the door filled the air with a flash of light and smoke. A satisfying pop sounded as the hatch was thrust from the side of the ship, crushing several bug soldiers in its wake.

"Mitsuki, run!" Guillermo screamed.

A barbed hairless tail shot from the darkness of the cargo hold and impaled a curious bug soldier, but that was all Guillermo dared see as he quickly sprinted away and grabbed Mitsuki who was fighting her way through soldiers to his right. The whiptails now began to emerge like cockroaches from the hold, their jaws gnashing at bug soldiers and their tails striking with paralytic venom. Each had been fitted with a black metallic collar that gleamed in the morning sun filtering through the mine entrance.

They better be right about the collars, crull it all.

Guillermo joined Mitsuki after grabbing up a couple of plasma rifles. He handed one to her and they began putting them to use, falling back behind a stack of supply crates as the chaos ensued. The bugs were more concerned with dealing with the whiptails than trying to subdue their Terran enemies, but they were indeed organized. A column of them began to form quickly as if hearing a silent cadence. In unison they fired at each whiptail, the combined power of their plasma rifles able to drop some of the smaller ones with ease. The two Terrans began firing into the column, but the bugs who fell were quickly replaced.

One of the whiptails charged Mitsuki, razor-mouth gnashing, and she raised the rifle in response. It bit down on the rifle just as she pulled the trigger effectively opening its head from behind.

She flashed a glance at Guillermo, her mouth drawn down in a grimace.

Guillermo's built-in wrist comm crackled to life.

"Have you placed the snare? We witnessed your bravery. Is the payload delivered?"

Guillermo fired a rapid shot at two of the bugs and dropped them.

"Yes, Zuraal," he said, the sweat plastering his hair into his eyes. "The beasties are doing their job, but they could be more of a problem for us if you don't zap them like you said you'd do."

"We descend on ropes to the mouth of the mine," came the staticky response, and the comm disconnected.

Guillermo and Mitsuki had switched to automatic on the plasma rifles and were dropping bug soldiers as well, but the bugs seemed unfazed by the losses, and the whiptails were still causing a chaotic mess. One of the biggest of the blue creatures, one that had been particularly hard to wrangle into the ship earlier that day, finally emerged from the hold, its body squeezing out of the hatch, its thick dorsal spines clicking against the metal as it moved. It immediately grabbed up three of the bugs in its jaws and swallowed them whole.

"Mamma's here," Guillermo said with a grin.

Mitsuki shushed him with a hiss, just as two of the smaller whiptails turned from the fray and noticed the two Terrans hiding behind the crates.

"I knew this plan was a crulling mistake," Guillermo growled, firing off a volley at one of them.

The two whiptails, each twice as long as Guillermo, crouched low to the tarmac, then charged forward on their powerful legs, their onyx claws clattering across the hardened surface.

"You ready?" Guillermo asked.

Mitsuki only furrowed her brow in silence.

CHAPTER 20

As the two-meter-long whiptails closed in on Guillermo and Mitsuki, the monsters began to slow, each of them circling to the left and to the right, a concerted effort to head off any escape. Guillermo could see them working out how to best kill their prey. He switched his plasma rifle to its highest emitter setting and waited for it to spin up while Mitsuki set her feet firmly and did the same. Before the weapons could reach full potential, however, the first whiptail, its jagged mouth gnashing, darted forward and leaped on top of the crate the Terrans were using for cover. It reached down with a clawed foot to slash at Guillermo, knocking the rifle from his grip and causing it to bounce across the tarmac.

Why didn't they give me the trigger device for the collars?!

Mitsuki reacted, shoving her rifle into its gaping jaws and pulling the trigger. The rifle leaked a gout of superheated plasma from its damaged power coil and melted a hole through the bottom jaw of the beast, then through the crate and into the slow-reactive thruster fuel within.

A tongue of yellow flame shot out of the crate, then the crate exploded.

Guillermo tried to shield Mitsuki with his body, but the two Terrans and the whiptails were sent flying in separate directions.

Mitsuki groaned, her black Ontoccan uniform wet

with her blood, and Guillermo could feel the sting of his own flesh from shrapnel and the sizzling heat of the explosion. He dared not look at his own injuries, trying to drag Mitsuki to safety through the chaos, but his right leg was not responding properly. He couldn't speak, and Mitsuki's eyes rolled as she opened her mouth and began to convulse. He scanned the tarmac for a medical kit, a med-station, anything that he could use to stabilize her. Sweat began to drip into his eye, and then he realized that it was not sweat but blood. He shook it off, grabbing at her shredded clothing with his mechanical hand. The arm was now a metallic endoskeleton, the rubberized sheath melted away and hanging in strips like rubber bands.

He heard another explosion, somewhere nearby, and through the blinding light of the entrance saw the familiar black uniform of Ontoccan soldiers of all races of the Five Rims. They rappelled from the cliffs above the entrance down into the mine, a few Fraaz taking wing. Their plasma guns fired streaks of blue light into the darkness. The soldiers dropped to the tarmac and began to also physically engage the bug soldiers. The whiptails, who had considerably thinned the ranks of the bugs, noticed as well. Some of the creatures broke away from the bugs to approach the new threat.

"Mitsuki," Guillermo said, returning his focus to her. "Can you hear me?"

She didn't respond, her eyes wide, her mouth open in a constant hyperventilating gasp. Her hands pressed against her chest as the blood oozed from a deep wound. His clothing, crinkled and blackened, was proof that he had shielded her from the flame, but not the shrapnel that had apparently worked its way past him.

"Mitsuki!" he shouted, pulling her along to a transport ship a few dozen meters away.

Perhaps he could get her in there, find a medical kit, a stasis pod, something to save her from this blunder of fate.

His right leg protested again, the pain in his ankle unbearable, and he took half a second to look at it.

His foot was cocked to the side at a weird angle.

No blood gushed from the wound, and if he had been lacerated it had probably been cauterized in the flames, but he could not stand. He felt the pain after realizing the injury, but he shook his head, gritted his teeth, and shouted a string of curses before dragging Mitsuki toward the waiting ship, grinding his ankle on the hard tarmac.

Another explosion rocked the hangar, then a vibrating hum as the collars were finally activated on the whiptails. Guillermo watched as the beasts all seized in convulsive pain, uttering brief squeals before falling motionless. The Ontoccans began to mop up the rest of the bug soldiers, but the enemy was intent on escaping in their ships and were charging forward.

Guillermo rasped for help, and the looming shape of Zuraal appeared from a cloud of grey smoke, his black eyes locking on the Terrans as he holstered his massive pistol. He loped on all six appendages, his tusked mouth open and onyx eyes wide as he scooped up the two of them and carried them across the tarmac. He lay them in the safety of an archway on the far side that connected to another large interior landing pad.

Gingerly he arranged them on the tarmac, his upper hands poised beside his head as he gritted his heavy teeth.

"My charges," he mumbled. "No plahuud on the altar today."

Guillermo was too dazed to try to decipher the Guajii-slang.

"Ring the bell clearly!" Guillermo shouted above the plasma bolts whizzing by.

The Guajiin did not answer, but only bounded away, drawing his pistol as he went, the massive bullets booming like cannon fire on an ancient battlefield. Guillermo lay still, listening to Mitsuki's unsteady breathing, and then he spotted a medical kit on the wall nearby. With some effort he managed to climb along with his hands as his right eye began to swell shut. He fumbled with the emergency release and the kit fell to the floor. Glancing through the doorway one more time he saw that the Ontoccans were winning the day, but some of the bug craft were lifting off and escaping, the plasma bolts of the Ontoccan soldiers chasing after them.

He focused on Mitsuki, dumping the contents of the

kit to the hard floor, scattering a few necessary bandages and equipment around before grasping a surgical stasis cauterizer. She screamed as he clamped it over the wound. As the device injected her with bio-mimetic sealer, her legs writhed and her heels scraped the floor. He then found a sedative, injected her with it, and she finally began to calm down, her breathing slowing to normal.

He lay beside her as he started to black out, but he fought it, clenched his teeth, and grunted an angry and determined string of hatred toward anyone who would listen. He used the blinding anger to keep him conscious.

Soon she began to stir, one eye opening and staring at him, the white of her eye filling with blood.

"Don't die on me, Mitsuki," Guillermo whispered. "I'm not crulling losing you."

The corner of her mouth twisted into a barely noticeable smirk and she coughed a few times before curling up into a fetal position next to him. He wrapped his arms around her and both of them lay on the floor, holding each other until they could no longer hear the sound of plasma rifles.

When Zuraal returned, one large hand holding a wounded side, Mitsuki had fallen asleep.

CHAPTER 21

An Ontoccan scout watched through the scope of his missile launcher as the last escaping bug fighter made a fiery hole in the canopy far below the hangar entrance. The collars were removed from the whiptails and then there was a concerted effort to lower them to the jungle floor below and not be eaten by them. Even in slumber the whiptail was armed with razor-sharp talons and hard spines along their back that made their transport difficult, but the Ontoccans managed well. The remaining ships, those not damaged in the initial battle, were a good haul for the Ontoccans as several fighters and a few gunships remained undamaged. Their engineers would have a difficult task trying to figure out the strange new tech. Several of the modified Terran craft could be repaired with time, but Zuraal was concerned about rallying to take the nearby Ontocca City back from the bugs within the next few days as he had been ordered.

The Ontoccan leadership was demanding, and they were severely outnumbered.

As Zuraal oversaw the removal of the whiptails and the repair work necessary to outfit all the remaining fighters he wondered why his superiors were so concerned with taking a city not terribly strategic to victory.

Yalrykk and Jupriish were particularly pushy about it.

Meanwhile, Guillermo and Mitsuki lay in a med-bay, each on their own stasis beds where Mitsuki was receiving expert medical care from an Aldrassan doctor whose bedside manner was a combination of highly skilled physician and superstitious ju-ju priest. The medic had erected small piles of feathers and bones in the med-bay to honor the gods of old while he used the most sophisticated medical equipment the Terrans had left behind after the war. Much of the equipment, however, was old and in dire need of repair. It had to be coaxed once in a while with extra presses of nimble fingers on control studs that didn't quite register the first time.

"Your injuries were not as severe as we first surmised, Terran," said Doctor Lahruud, his last name pronounced by rolling the "r". "It seems that the nanites in your system are already rebuilding the tendons in your foot and you should be able to use it within a few days. I have fitted a brace on the ankle and connected it to the bone as to allow your tendons and muscles to knit themselves back together. Amazing devices these nanites, even if they have…side effects. Your mechanical arm has been given a full workup and is thankfully repaired. However, I would suggest you do not walk on the brace for a cycle. I have luckily procured this repulser chair which is hopefully to your liking."

"Doc…it'll be…great, I guess," Guillermo replied, adjusting himself in the bed. Guillermo's nanotech system never ceased to amaze him, healing him from some of the worst injuries, but it did not dull the pain. And there were indeed side effects. He absently wondered if he would grow back his head if it were blown off.

"Your friend is different story, I am afraid. A shard of metal has wedged itself very near her heart, and since we have not the technology to reach it safely, I have placed her in stasis until we can procure the proper equipment. She will need greater treatment than I can provide here. I am indeed praying for her. Also, her DNA signature is…odd. I am not sure what to make of it."

"What do you mean her DNA was 'odd'?"

"Something is not right about it, and the equipment we have is not capable of reading the flaw. I am certain her health is otherwise not at risk, that is if we remove the shard, but if she were to require a skin graft or a limb replacement, any cloning would be unsuccessful. All tissue samples failed to germinate."

Guillermo winced as he sat up in the bed to face Lahruud.

"They said the same thing about me when they gave me the nanites and this arm. But the nanites are able to repair me. You could give her some of my blood…"

"We have not the technology to do such a thing. The risks are too great. All of that tech is in the facility in Ontocca City, and it is currently occupied by the enemy."

"But my partner. She was a bug. They worked with her."

The Aldrassan's skin flushed.

"I do not want to risk it in her case. The nanites are able to reconstruct your cells on a molecular level by using material from your own body…basically they only accelerate your healing. It is not a healthy fix, and I feel that the physician who originally performed this procedure on you was flawed in judgement. Your nanites come with a price, Guillermo. They rob your body of certain nutrients and from my latest scans of you I now understand why this type of thing was abandoned by the Phaedran Empire."

"What do you mean?" Guillermo asked, his hand forming a fist that wadded the bedding.

"I am not certain," replied the doctor. "But it seems that you are living a life of a fast-burning candle. We cannot remove the nanites, as they have bonded to your physiology, but if you continue to be injured and repaired in this way you will shorten your life span considerably. If you will slow down, not injure yourself further, you could live a normal life for a Terran."

Guillermo turned his head and stared at Mitsuki, her eyelids purple and bruised from the concussion of the explosion, her chest wrapped in a tight bandage that covered the wound close to her heart.

"What can I do?" Guillermo asked, his eyes narrowing.

"As stated, I am not capable of reversing the damage done by the so-called doctors who —"

"No," Guillermo said, his cold gaze falling on the doctor. "Not about me...about her."

"I am sorry, my friend," Doctor Lahruud said, folding his six fingered hands. "If we could get her to Ontocca City we could take advantage of the more advanced Terran tech. I am quite limited here."

"Then we have to get her there."

The Aldrassan's eyes flicked once and he raised his strange hands as if being held at gunpoint.

"Currently that city, as I said, is being held by the bug armies. Zuraal is devising a plan to take it back as ordered by Yalrykk, but it will take much more time than we have to restore her to full health."

Guillermo sat up in bed, pushing off the mattress and sliding to the floor. He winced when he placed his braced foot on the smooth black surface.

"I don't give a whiptail's nugget what Zuraal is planning and how long," Guillermo growled as Dr. Lahruud struggled to steady him, trying to force him back into the bed. "If I've got precious little time left, I'll spend it trying to survive, save Mitsuki at least. A few days ago I thought I was the last of my kind, but now I found her, and I'm hoping there are probably more of us out there. The quicker I help you Ontoccans oust the bugs the quicker I get on to finding my partner and more Terrans like me."

Guillermo stood shakily, steadying himself with one hand on the bed.

"Get me to Zuraal," he said. "I have a few ideas of my own."

"Rest the sleep of the dead, Terran," came the booming voice of Zuraal as he strode through the door, a bandage wrapped tightly around his midsection. "Bind you in the thrall of the huuzraan if do not comply, you."

Guillermo furrowed his brow.

"Want to see this arm perform a wicked uppercut?"

The Guajiin rested one hand on the carved handle of his half-meter long revolver, then locked his eyes with Guillermo in a reflexive stance that was instinctual. Guajiin were born fighters, ready to accept any challenge, but after a strange smile spread across Zuraal's face his four arms went slack.

"Greater puzzles have I than your nurse-care," Zuraal said, attempting a smile. "Rest in the cool of the meadow."

Guillermo complied, easing onto the bed, a grumble heard softly which blended with the respirator machines keeping Mitsuki in an induced coma.

"We have to get Mitsuki to a hospital in Ontocca City, Zuraal. Somehow."

The Guajiin's gaze fell on the doctor who smiled strangely, his tiny sharp teeth visible.

"Vacate," Zuraal said, and the Doctor bowed quietly and then shuffled out of the room.

CHAPTER 22

When the door closed, Zuraal's face grew grave, his large lips pressing together faintly as if he had something to tell Guillermo, something that he had wanted to say for some time, but had not the courage to do. He turned, strode to the door to enter a lock code, then returned to sit on an empty bed between the door and Guillermo. The bed creaked beneath his weight.

Before he spoke, he let out an over-long sigh, Guajiin lung capacity being what it is, and then rested his two lower arms on his knees and folded his upper arms.

"Of your parentage," Zuraal said, nudging Guillermo's shoulder with a large finger. "Tell the tale."

"I...was born on the bug world," Guillermo replied, his mouth twisting. "Why do you ask?"

Zuraal stood suddenly, paced the floor, his lower arms on his hips, his upper arms gesticulating with his speech.

"The female, could you remember-draw her face? Mitsuki?"

"No...well, sort of. You mean, have I seen her

before meeting her in the jungle? I don't know. Not really."

"What if remember-drawing is hidden, as prey in the bush, and I could reveal the way to ensnare it?" asked Zuraal, his upper hands outstretched. "I have watch-cared over you since days of old, blood-oath I made. I could remember-draw your face...and I swore on the blood of the ancestors for the mission to be complete... but I have lost my way. I risked all in bringing babes through the ion storm-cloud. The enclave gone. The Shibboleth lost. Hide you in mother's arms I did. I could not hold in my victory-shout, for my heart is warmed by the fire of your life-knowledge."

Guillermo held up his hand as if to block the speech from Zuraal's mouth.

"What in the great Aldrassan gulf are you yammering about, Zuraal? Ring the bell clearly, or whatever. So...you know Mitsuki and I? Let me see if I understand you right. You brought us here from some other place when we were babies? I can get most of what you said, but what is a Shibboleth?"

The Guajiin looked behind him and then back at Guillermo as if he were sharing a terrible secret, almost instinctually as if he were being watched. His large mouth turned down and his small black eyes narrowed.

"Shibboleth is sacred and hidden, but found not to
be safe. Locust Phaedrans seek to quell their family
line. When out of your mother's womb you came, I
chose the mission by pain of death…from the Phaedran
Empire, after the culling, through the sparkly ion
storm-cloud…and swore a blood oath to keep you from
them, from the talking locusts who eat worlds."

Guillermo could only stare at Zuraal, his mind
trying to decipher the Guaji-slang. He didn't know if
he was hearing Zuraal correctly, but from the pieces of
what he understood he began to puzzle together the
truth. He probed further.

"Tell me everything," he said. "You went beyond the
ion cloud? The barrier? How? It has shattered every
ship that has tried to pass it."

"In the dawn-days of my life-path I scrounged…"

"You were a salvager?"

"Yes," Zuraal continued. "At the edge of the Five
Rims boundary, near the ionic storm-cloud I spied and
a litter of…salvage… a metal graveyard it was, the
remnant of the Phaedran ship cast there by our Five
Rim brothers."

"Yes," Guillermo offered. "The Phaedran world

ships that didn't make it through the barrier broke up or were severely damaged as they were forced to go through."

"Such was my mind-story, too. I gathered the precious shinies, but then a star appeared to port, a flash of light, and I woke in a cage, was bond-slave to Phaedrans who were not the same...changed somehow...bigger...taller."

Guillermo remembered the woman who had appeared to him in the Queen's chamber so long ago, how she killed the entire Ontoccan delegation and the Queen before disappearing into a chrome, spheroid wormhole.

He decided to risk full disclosure.

"I saw one...a Phaedran, I guess," Guillermo said, his voice low. "Back on the bug world, in the Queen's chamber. She had some kind of personal cloak that masked who she really was. Was masquerading as the Queen's Aldrassan aide. She killed the Ontoccan delegates and the Queen. She attacked so suddenly that I didn't have time to react, and before I knew it she had paralyzed me with a crulling beam and then disappeared into a portable wormhole. I've never seen anything like it."

Zuraal shifted his weight from one foot to the other and frowned.

"Their tech is quicker-duel than ours," Zuraal said. "I fear they have glow-minded a path through the sparkly ion storm-cloud. Quake I in my skin. The duel shall be great, us."

"The Terran woman said something about destabilizing the Five Rims governments…That they, the Phaedrans, were working toward revenge. She seemed really unfazed by my attempt to stop her."

Guillermo saw that Zuraal was formulating thoughts in his own language, his face contorting to try to verbalize his concern. Guillermo held up a hand to stay him.

"I've spent every moment of spare time trying to piece together who she was," Guillermo confessed, then his face grew grave. "You say that you brought us here? Mitsuki and I? Through the ionic barrier. How did you get through it?"

Zuraal straightened, his face warming with a wry smile.

"By the grace of the maker," he said as if that answered all questions. "And a looted craft, sail unfurled."

"You came here in a Phaedran ship?"

"Made the journey, then offered it on the altar of death. No tracks to be found for the hunting. The Phaedran locusts be confounded in a swamp of questions. It is as I was commanded by the blood-oath of the Shibboleth."

Mitsuki stirred, a soft moan escaping her swollen lips. Guillermo glanced at her stasis bed and then continued.

"You were on the Phaedran world? They obviously survived the exile…and you ended up there? How? And again with this Shibboleth. I'm not understanding —"

"I spin the story again, Guillermo. A bright sun appeared to port, and then I woke in a cage, then in slavery bound was I, for some time, made to duel without my d'shaaluud in the great hall of death… against their machines."

He pointed to his half-meter long revolver, sadness in his dark eyes.

"This one crafted I with much sadness born, the other lost to the ages, and shame hunts my path for its loss."

"So the Phaedrans captured you? You were made

to fight…like gladiatorial bouts?"

Zuraal nodded.

"And then the trail grows fresh anew," Zuraal said, nodding affirmatively. "Green again, the Shibboleth, hidden in plain sight, stole me away to their home, placed me in the cleft of the rock, safe in mother's arms…for that I am in blood-debt to them."

"So there is a rebellion on the Phaedran world? That's the Shibboleth, right?" Guillermo asked, and the old Guajiin smiled and placed a hand on Guillermo's knee. The fingers felt like rough stones.

"They gift the Five Rims with your life-blood, Guillermo," Zuraal said. "I have hidden the two of you well, the children of the Shibboleth, the two whose blood holds the key. Within your bones the answer lies. And safe there it waits until the appointed time. The eyes and ears of the enemy track us through the bush. The tale of the Phaedran woman you spin chills the bone and my hope is tested with this news."

Guillermo listened intently then as Zuraal told him more. As far as he could tell Zuraal spoke of a remnant of Terrans who rode with the Phaedran Terrans on one of the world ships, hoping that they could redeem their race. It failed, and they were hunted, but then they escaped to an island on a planet just at the edge of the ion storm barrier. From there they planned to infiltrate the Phaedran Empire, but the Phaedrans were growing in power and advancing their technology. Through the haze of Zuraal's Guaji-slang Guillermo deciphered that the Phaedrans were under the leadership of a new enemy, someone he called the "Old One", and when he spoke about it a terrible fear washed across his eyes.

After gaining all the information he could stomach, Guillermo placed a hand on Zuraal's meaty shoulder.

"Well, we can catch up on old family stories some other time," he said. "Right now we have an assault on Ontocca City to plan.

"Yalrykk is honor-bound to take Ontocca City, but the capital is the greater prize," Zuraal replied. "His reasoning is not for me to question, but I am lost in the fog. Waiting for your flag on the horizon, Guillermo. Replenished are you?"

"Yeah yeah," Guillermo said. "Whatever, pal. I'm sure Yalrykk has his reasons for wanting to take such a minor target right now…probably our numbers. Anyway, I'm as good as I'm going to be, so let's get to it. I have a few ideas."

CHAPTER 23

A few days later, his ankle now only sore, they began the trek through the jungle toward Ontocca City.

He piloted a transport ship to within ten kilometers and set down in a clearing after scanning the foliage for any roaming teams of whiptails. Strangely there were not any bug patrols as yet. Zuraal seemed to think that their forces were still not reinforced enough for organized and systematic fly-overs.

As Guillermo powered down the ship and began post-flight checks to ensure a speedy lift-off, he fell into the mundane tasks of silencing the engines and cycling the energy cells. This caused his mind to roll and toss with the overload of terrible news he had been given. To find out that his parents were not his true parents, that he apparently had been born beyond the ionic cloud, and that he had been spirited here by a former smuggler who ended up at the wrong place at the wrong time. It was nearly too much to stomach. Not to mention the fact that the microscopic robots that had so often saved his life were also shortening his life span. He decided to ask Zuraal more questions when they had figured out a way to get Mitsuki cured, and he hoped that their new and even more desperate plan would work to secure Ontocca City.

"Web is woven," Zuraal said, sticking his over-large head through the cockpit door. "Armies allied in wait of orders. Perhaps we will be quicker on the draw."

"Perhaps," Guillermo responded, his hands moving over the controls, the engines growing quiet. "Or we'll all die trying."

The elephant in the room silenced them for a moment.

"It's all too unbelievable," Guillermo offered.

"We dance on the edge of the cliff," Zuraal responded.

"No, no," Guillermo replied. "I mean about what you told me...about the Phaedran Empire beyond the ionic barrier. I'm still trying to get my head around it."

Zuraal twisted his mouth in a grim expression.

"My commanders are blind to it," he said. "They think me of brain-rot."

The big Guajiin helped Guillermo out of his chair and aided him slightly as they exited the ship along the landing ramp where a rabble of battle-weary Ontoccans stood waiting. Each of them, Fraaz, Guajiin, Aldrassan and bug alike stood at attention, their weapons slung for the trek to the ridge overlooking the city. Zuraal gave the command to move out with a hand-signal that everyone understood, but Guillermo could read even on the alien faces the gravity of their situation.

They were outnumbered, headed to an uncertain and dangerous coordinated attack, and as usual their tenacity would have to outweigh the odds. It did not help morale that Ontocca City was not a major target. However, it held the stockpile of old Terran tech, a more valuable target for their leaders.

Orders were orders.

As they snaked through the underbrush Guillermo traveled close to one of Zuraal's lieutenants, an Aldrassan hunter named Jupriish. Jupriish, an Ontoccan geneticist with a penchant for living rather tribal, had been instrumental in procuring all of the whiptails for use on the initial attack on the mine. He had arrived late to the battle because he had chosen to scale the cliffs himself to the mouth of the hangar bay without ropes or any technological equipment. He was part of a sect of Aldrassan priests who had their roots in Aldrassan history long before the arrival of the Phaedran Empire, a group who were instrumental in the original rebellion against the Terrans. Apparently he was also a genetic genius, his involvement with the Ontoccan government a "high value asset", as Yalrykk had explained, even if his demeanor was off-putting. As they traveled, Jupriish would stop now and again, hold up a six-fingered hand for them to wait, and then would proceed after listening intently. His understanding of Ontoccan wildlife was, as Guillermo had been told, "second to none".

Guillermo found him otherwise cold but decided to figure him out in his usual way, which was by being an annoyance.

He sidled up to the Aldrassan, who wore nothing but a simple loin-cloth and carried a gnarled spear covered in drab yellow feathers. Guillermo opened his mouth to speak, but Jupriish turned his head and answered before the Terran could utter a sound.

"It is best if you do not distract me," said Jupriish. "This part of the jungle is unforgiving to those who do not respect it."

"I...respect it, old guy," Guillermo said, a curt smile on his lips. "I just thought I'd make small talk. It'll be a long hike."

The Aldrassan stopped, took one step toward

Guillermo so that he was uncomfortably close, and leaned in to sniff the air centimeters away from Guillermo's nose.

"All I need to know about you is what I can smell," Jupriish said flatly. "And that is obviously not of consequence to this mission. Your presence is not required, and truth be told you are an asset we would rather not have on the front lines. Now let me do my job, and try not to get killed. We need you, Terran, if this is going to work. Especially if it doesn't."

Jupriish moved away, but in a few moments Zuraal stood beside Guillermo, a heavy hand falling on the Terran's shoulder. Guillermo couldn't figure out what the Aldrassan meant by that last comment, but now he had to decipher Guajii-slang.

"It is a foul wind that warns of future slaughter," said Zuraal. "It is best you heed the scent."

Guillermo laughed a little too loud.

"Now *that* I understand. How much farther?"

"The summit is our destiny," Zuraal said, moving past him.

Guillermo's ankle was aching tremendously, but not enough to keep him from his goal. Mitsuki had to get the help she needed, and she was not going to heal properly without the equipment in the Ontocca City hospital, that was sure, or so he had been told. He fought through the pain and continued on.

After several kilometers of unforgiving jungle vines and thorns they emerged at the incline that led to the summit of the ridge. Jupriish guided them along, and Guillermo did not interrupt him anymore in his quest to see to their safety. Several times they had to stop, crouching low in the foliage as a troop of whiptails passed by, Jupriish using a slimy substance from a leathery sack to spread on the leaves around them to ward the beasts away. Whatever it was smelled sickening sweet, but it caused the whiptails to take one sniff of it before chittering out a warning call and crashing through the trees to escape.

Guillermo decided that he had to get some of that stuff, that is if he could manage not to reflex-gag every time he caught wind of it.

As they approached the summit the rocks became larger and more jagged, and his ankle was beginning to ache and throb even though the nanites were probably hard at work repairing it. They crouched low, the group of Guajiin in their number crawling along on all six appendages, and Jupriish scouted ahead to disappear over the rise. They all waited quietly as they heard the distant approach of a flying craft, and soon three bug fighters hummed overhead, rocketing by them and down the slope of the mountain, hugging the tops of the trees. Soon Jupriish emerged, his spear in front of him, and he displayed no visible emotion in his report to Zuraal.

"It is worse than we thought," Jupriish said, his large eyelids flicking over opaque irises. "They have fortified the city with some kind of tower guns that rise above the canopy. They are erecting something atop the dome of the city as well, the purpose of which I cannot determine. If we are to attack them we must do it immediately. We must capture the technology facility. Our defense depends on it."

"Could I have a look at it?" Guillermo asked.

The Aldrassan pursed his lips, a sign of disrespect.

"The pilot wishes to be a general, then," said Jupriish. "Perhaps you should relinquish command to it. And why is it not waiting at the mine?"

"Unity through diversity," Zuraal said, his voice gravelly. "You will comply. *He* is a key to the lock of victory."

"My pheromonal bomb will be the key to our victory, not some Terran," Jupriish countered. "We have to get it to the center of the city in order to confuse the enemy. Then we will be able to take back what is ours."

"Move at the right time or scare the prey," Zuraal said, placing a heavy hand on Guillermo's shoulder. "Our allies will help us win the day."

The Aldrassan skulked away, climbing back to the summit to crouch in the undergrowth.

"What the chert is he on about?" Guillermo said.

"His order is splintered, forever broken by the Phaedran of old," Zuraal said. "Forgiveness does not exit his door to greet you. But he is on the trail of victory. His pheromonal bomb will be our high tower of safety."

Guillermo did not respond, but only pulled his plasma rifle from his shoulder and trekked up the mountain to eventually emerge at the summit and then stare down at the city. He could see the ancient Terran world ship that the Ontoccans had transformed into the hub for a thriving city. The world ship, a colossal rusting mushroom cap, rose from a cluster of skyscrapers that were dwarfed by the ancient vessel.

Even from this distance Guillermo could see the towers Jupriish had described. Dotting the hull of the world ship were several hundred bug landing craft and gunships, a hive of buzzing hornets waiting for some unlucky attacker to disturb them. Guillermo pointed at the trapezoidal structure on top of the dome.

"Is that what you were talking about, Jupriish? The black structure?"

"Of course, Terran," Jupriish said flatly. "It is a variable not discussed in the original plan. This will be difficult. You should not be here. Pheromonal bomb or not this will be a hard fight."

Guillermo turned to the Aldrassan and grinned.

"My life has been a list of unplanned variables, pal. I've never backed down from a fight."

Jupriish only bared his teeth, not really a smile but a signal of understanding, and soon Zuraal and the others were crouching nearby.

"Soothsay the battle words, Guillermo," Zuraal said. "We are your underlings."

Guillermo produced a small pair of range-finding binocs and peered through them at the city below. He saw what he had hoped would be there and then motioned for Zuraal to come closer.

"See that egg shaped building just this side of the reclamation plant?" Guillermo said as he handed the binocs to Zuraal. "You see that contingent of bug shock troops near the egg-shaped thing? They have several hover vehicles outfitted with what look like plasma cannons, but I'm not really sure. That tech isn't Terran in origin, so I've got no idea what it does or how to disable it. I think our best bet is to take out the southern reactor and that will buy us enough time to get the bomb to the city center."

Zuraal pulled the binocs away from his eyes, his mouth open.

"A hedge of thorns surrounds the quarry," said the Guajiin. "We have the low ground in this battle."

"Yeah. No kidding. I think if we can be stealthy about it, maybe dress as refugees returning to their homes for supplies we can get close enough to the reactor to take it out. If Jupriish and his squad can then use that opportunity to get to the center of the city then that might be enough to get us poised to take down the rest of them."

"This plan is lacking one key element," Jupriish offered.

"What is that?" Guillermo asked.

The Aldrassan pointed at a spire just to the left of the main reactor.

"A plan B as your kind would say," said Jupriish. "That spire could be another nexus for the bomb to do its work, but it will not allow us to cover the entire city with the pheromone."

"Good thinking Jupriish," Guillermo continued. "We will hit the reactor, but if we fail, you can climb the spire to release the pheromone there."

"Eyes within the enemy's ranks, have we," Zuraal offered. "Our bug brethren have sacrificed much to betray their ancestors."

Guillermo's expression became grave.

"If your guys in the city can be ready," he said. "We can hopefully take out any opposition before they have time to react."

Zuraal peered through the binocs again.

"Near the southern reactor the enemy is strong in number," Zuraal said, then handed Guillermo the binocs.

"Yeah," said Guillermo, his face slack. "I guess you'll leave that one up to me. I'll need a couple of stealthy guys. Who do you have?"

Zuraal turned his head and landed his gaze on

three Aldrassans who were squatting in the dirt, their hard gaze boring a hole in Guillermo.

"Well chert," Guillermo said. "I guess I don't have a choice. You ready to play ball, fellas?"

One of the Aldrassans stood, folding his six-fingered hands together in front of him and closing his eyes as if in prayer.

"All hope is in our mission to succeed, Terran," said the Aldrassan. "I will comply to your leadership for now, and entrust my brother Jupriish to deliver the bomb to its destination. But you must be careful. If you die we are lost."

"I don't plan on dying today, but glad to have your vote of confidence there, skinny. Let's go."

CHAPTER 24

Seventy or so strong of Ontoccan defense fighters gathered in the refugee camp just at the outskirts of Ontocca City, each of them dressed in common attire. The only one of them who stood out was Guillermo, standing among them as if he were one of their number. He had covered his face with a scarf and wore a wide-brimmed hat, but deep down he felt like this fool's errand would be the one that would get him killed.

Of course he always felt like that.

They had assured him that once they had taken the city Mitsuki would be flown in to the hospital where the doctor could begin to remove the shard, but the shaky nature of their plan worried him.

Zuraal stood in the middle of them, a steaming cup of j'umaa in his hand, and a face hardened by determination.

"We lay the snare for the prize prey, hunters," he said, his voice low and gravelly. "Each to each your path has been laid. Leaders take your prize warriors under wing."

Guillermo had been placed in charge of a five

member commando team made up of two bug engineers and three Aldrassan toughs whose normal primitive nature looked out of place with their battle armor and slung plasma rifles. Each of the Aldrassans carried a ceremonial bone knife on their hip, the dried blood of the weapon's last kill visible along the edge of the blade. The two bug engineers whom Guillermo had affectionately labeled "Nerd One" and "Nerd Two" fiddled with tools in their tool bags in a procedure that he could only assume were like his own pre-flight checks.

The Aldrassans were a little easier to figure out. Their glares were legendary.

"Perhaps Jupriish is punishing us by placing us under your command, Terran," said Gyaanik, the larger of the three.

"A means to an end," Guillermo smiled. "I help you take out the reactor. You take back your city. I get my friend the medical attention she needs. Now swallow the negativity and fall in line."

Gyaanik clicked his tongue and hissed, a sign unknown to Guillermo but nothing he thought was positive. Guillermo informed his squad that they had been ordered to take down the security shield that surrounded the reactor. After this, a squadron of fighters would run interference while another squadron or two would hit the reactor with a plasma bomb. They had been assured that the damage would be minimal, but would shut down the power to the city so that the pheromonal bomb could be smuggled in. Then their ground forces, backed up by able bodied refugees, would have a better chance at dominating the confused bug forces.

"A solid plan," said Vuudsh, one of the Aldrassans. "If the dreadnaught doesn't come to their assistance."

"It's a risk we have to take," Guillermo replied. "I have to get to that hospital at least. You can have your crulling city."

"What is a Mitsuki?" asked Fuudqis, another Aldrassan.

"One of mine, and that's all you need to know."

"We are blood-bound to this resistance, Terran. We do not expect you to understand our loyalties. Only know that even though we despise your race, we will work with you to our common goal to remove this scourge from our world."

"Good enough, I guess," Guillermo laughed.

Now come on."

They passed several units of soldiers who were gearing up for other strikes against the city, and then worked their way around the large communication jammers that emitted a high pitched frequency, blocking the bug armada from seeing their weapon signatures. Guillermo knew that once they emerged from the jungle and entered the outer suburbs of the city their weapons would be noticed on sensor sweeps, and he was prepared for that.

"Take out your power cells," he ordered, and his small unit complied. "The scanners pick up active power signatures, so if our guns aren't loaded, they will have nothing to track."

Each Aldrassan took their bone knives in hand even though they were still a good distance from the city. Guillermo was somehow comforted by this show, but carried a small projectile weapon in his jacket pocket just in case.

They trekked through the jungle, the Aldrassans scouting ahead as they moved, and he began to smell the odor of a pheromone that he recognized from his time with Dervish. The Nerds were attempting to mask their presence, a pheromone that Jupriish had reengineered to be spread all over the city. Ontoccan bug soldiers were taking on more menial tasks for this mission.

As they emerged from the jungle and crossed a two-lane road where several hover-vehicles sat idle, they noticed that not a soul was visible, not even the bug soldiers that usually patrolled this area. The hair on Guillermo's arm raised and an energy blast crackled the air less than a few centimeters from his head.

His group shifted focus, taking cover behind a low wall on the other side of the street as more of the deadly bolts flew by, some of them connecting with the plasticrete and shattering it, sending little fragments of wall and street in every direction.

"Ambush!" growled Gyaanik, switching his knife from hand to hand. "As expected."

"Expected?" Guillermo countered. "You expected this? Why didn't you fill me in?"

The three Aldrassans ignored him, running away and ducking down a back alley leaving Guillermo and the two Nerds who were now slamming their energy packs back into their plasma rifles. After this was accomplished, the two bugs left Guillermo alone as well, running around the other side of the wall and back across the street toward an outbuilding where they soon disappeared from view, yellow plasma blasts following them all the way.

Guillermo slid his back down the wall, sat on the hard plasticrete, and fumbled for his own energy pack. He clumsily drove it home in the stock of his rifle. For a few seconds he listened to the plasma bolts ping off of hover-vehicles and explode more plasticrete shards in the air. With a primal scream he popped his head above the low wall and looked down the barrel of his rifle only to take cover again as a bolt struck the top of his hat and caught it on fire.

"You v'oshtu-loving…" was all he got out as he ripped the hat from his head and threw it away before ducking back behind the wall. He took a deep breath, sucking in and blowing out through pursed lips, then shot to his feet and ran toward the alleyway.

Five bug soldiers lay in the alley, their wounds deep and fatal.

"Chert," Guillermo muttered.

He stepped around them, then managed to find a side street where he cautiously hugged the wall of a nearby building, navigating back toward the main street. When he emerged from the alley, the plasma blasts had ended and his companions were standing in a small circle in the middle of the street. Each of them turned to face him as if it were an afterthought.

"Shall we continue?" asked Gyaanik as he sheathed his blade.

"Um, yeah…sure," Guillermo replied.

He joined them and they continued on, taking back alleys when possible, and as they came closer to their objective they dropped down a sewer grate and had to crouch low. Even though Nerd 1 and Nerd 2 had the most sensitive olfactory system they didn't let on, and Guillermo brought up the rear, scouting behind them for any unwelcome followers. The tunnel was low and dank, and Guillermo wrapped his scarf around his mouth and nose to filter out the overwhelming odor without much success. As they neared their destination, however, Vuudsh raised a six fingered hand and pointed ahead of them down the greasy tunnel.

"It is a snare," said Vuudsh, his accent thick. "Shaddan au'vrah."

Gyaanik nodded, his bottom lip protruding, then turned to the rest of the squad and let out a long sigh.

"We will have to go back," he said. "Approach the objective from the surface. We cannot reach through the energy field to shut down the snare as it will vaporize flesh."

Guillermo looked down the tunnel and flicked on a lamp at the end of his plasma rifle. Just beyond them a ripple effect was all that could be seen of a dangerous energy field, but just beyond that was a control panel. Without a word, Guillermo strode forward, reached through he field with his metallic arm, flipped a switch, and motioned everyone on.

"I guess you guys needed me after all," he chided. "Now let's get on with it."

There was a brief exchange of light laughter before they filed further down the tunnel. They eventually emerged in a large circular room where several streams of sewage poured in from various outlets on the walls, splashing the liquid on the floor and causing a spray of unpleasant droplets that soon covered them in a foul dampness.

"There," said Gyaanik, pointing at a grate far above them.

Nerd 2 pulled a small ascension gun out of his pack and fired at the grate. Soon they were climbing the sturdy micro-filament line to the surface where they emerged cautiously, only to find a deserted street and a sinking feeling that they were being watched.

Guillermo wiped his face with his damp scarf and tried not to make a sound as they scurried to a nearby alley to peer around a wall at the unmistakable shimmer of an energy shield. Any light escaping the shield was bent in such a way as to cause a telescoping effect on the terrain beyond it.

The Nerds went to work immediately, setting up their equipment as Guillermo and the Aldrassans took point, scanning the alleyway and the street for any sign of bug soldiers. Nerd 1 switched on the jammer that they had designed to take down the shield, and Guillermo looked down the street to see that the telescopic effect beyond the barrier was beginning to fluctuate and normalize.

He turned to look at Nerd 1 and smile, but when he turned back to look down the street there were twenty or so armored bug soldiers and a large lumbering vehicle plodding along via six robotic legs, bristling with guns.

An armored force was moving toward them.

CHAPTER 25

"We've got a problem," Guillermo said as calmly as he could manage. "Actually we've got about twenty problems headed this way…and…you know…a tank."

The three Aldrassans peered around the corner of the plasticrete wall and then turned around to give Guillermo blank stares as the Nerds furiously worked to assemble the shield jammer, the panel on the front of it mysteriously beginning to spark.

"Is that thing supposed to do that?" Guillermo asked.

Nerd 1 shook his head and continued working, then pulled his hand back suddenly as a spark shot out at him.

"Have they detected us?" asked Guillermo of the Nerds.

Both of them shrugged, and Fuudqis gave him a hasty "thumbs-up". Guillermo returned the gesture, his mouth a half-smile, and Gyaanik bumped Guillermo's elbow.

"We have to get the shield down so that the fighters will be able to bomb the power station," Gyaanik said, his voice even.

"Thanks Captain Obvious," Guillermo responded, his voice not so even. "How do you propose we do that?"

The Aldrassan set his mouth and shot a hard glance at his compatriots before turning back to Guillermo.

"There is a window in this building," said Gyaanik rapping his knuckles on a nearby wall. "It will allow us to gain a better view of the power station. Our techs must get to that window to set up the shield jammer. The closer the better. We need a diversion."

Guillermo took one more look around the corner, and now the giant mechanical beetle lumbering along within a column of bug soldiers who were marching in lockstep. His only thought was about Mitsuki, about the hospital which was only a few kilometers from here, and that he desperately needed to get her the help she needed.

"Right," Guillermo said as he leaned his back against the wall and took in a deep breath. "Didn't you guys bring some high explosive with you?"

"I do not understand what you mean," Gyaanik said. "We have the thermoplast to use in case the shield jammer fails, but it is not —"

"Exactly," Guillermo said, thrusting out his open hand. "Give it to me. Don't ask questions. Just give it to me."

Nerd 2 fumbled through his satchel and produced a small orb of thermaplast, hesitated, then pulled out a small detonator. Guillermo had to eventually snatch it from his hand.

"When I do this thing I'm going to try, I want you guys to go through this building here and get the jammer to that window. I'm going to be your crulling diversion."

"This is foolish," Gyaanik said, a hand on Guillermo's shoulder. "Let us do this thing. You are the last —"

"Again! Captain Obvious!" Guillermo growled, shoving the explosive in his jacket pocket and thumbing his plasma rifle to auto. "I don't plan on dying today."

With that he crouched low and moved out onto the street to squat behind a hover truck, the hum of its passive gravitic repulsers providing a half-meter gap beneath. Guillermo peered around the truck to see the strange six-legged vehicle plodding forward as the group of bug soldiers passed through the shield and began their patrol in his direction. The street was flanked by low buildings, all of them vacant of citizens after the evacuation. The street, lined on either side by derelict hover vehicles, was pock marked with ugly plasma burns. At least there wouldn't be any collateral casualties for what he was planning to do.

He took one final look at his crew in the alleyway, then motioned with his hand that they should get busy doing what he told them to do. The five of them didn't waste any time, but two of the Aldrassans, Vuudsh and Fuudqis, shot across the pavement to join him behind the truck.

"Crull it all, I told you to —"

"We must succeed," said Vuudsh, his voice a little more tinny than Gyaanik's. "The Commander is not as confident in your abilities as you seem to be."

Guillermo saw Gyaanik pull his blade and nod toward his men as he turned and followed the Nerds down the alley and out of sight.

"I guess we're on," Guillermo said, his voice cracking.

"On what?" asked Fuudqis, looking around at his feet.

Guillermo rolled his eyes, then peered around the side of the truck to see that the troop of bug soldiers and their ugly new weapon were getting closer, that they had cleared the shimmering shield wall and were now only twenty or so meters from the hover truck. Guillermo plucked the thermoplast sphere from his pocket and attached the small detonator switch, pressing it down into the soft explosive. He had only read about this kind of device in a training manual for the bug security force years ago.

Actually "skimmed" was a better word.

It was simple enough, however.

He looked at the ball in his hand for a moment, then handed it to Vuudsh.

"What should I do with this?" he asked.

"Ever play baseball?"

"No," said Vuudsh. "What is baseball?"

Guillermo hoped the Aldrassan could throw a fast ball.

"That tank is probably not impervious to explosives," Guillermo said. "When you see it get close enough, toss that thermaplast under the tank. Now give me your plasma rifle."

"But you already have one."

"I know," he said. "I need two."

Vuudsh shrugged and gave up his rifle, and

Guillermo took one in each hand, thumbing the new one over to automatic setting. He inhaled and exhaled three sharp breaths, squeezed his eyes shut briefly, then rolled out around the hover truck into the open.

"Alright you v'oshtus! Come to daddy!" Guillermo screamed as he ran across the street to a waiting hover vehicle, firing his plasma rifles blindly.

The bugs didn't react right away, about five of them slumping to the ground, felled by Guillermo's rapid blue plasma blasts. The six-legged robot beetle rotated antennae-shaped guns in Guillermo's direction and opened fire as the remainder of the bugs took cover behind derelict hover vehicles lining the street. Guillermo climbed into the driver's seat of a nearby vehicle, popping the cover from the control panel and hot-wiring the thing to life.

Even though the six-legged bug tank was intimidating, it was remarkably slow, its high powered energy cannons rotating around at a snail's pace. The bug soldiers, however, were a bit more successful, and the transparesteel window of the car exploded, sending little hot shards all over Guillermo's face and neck. He responded by opening the throttle on the car and pointing it toward the mechanized beetle.

The tank responded with a volley of blasts from its main cannon, and Guillermo rolled out onto the street just as the vehicle lit up the pavement, transforming into a fiery mess that littered debris in a scattered, burning pile. The smoke and fire of the crash created an instant barrier for the bug soldiers, but not for the beetle tank as it waddled through the orange flames and kicked scraps of metal along with its segmented legs.

But it was now alone.

"Throw the ball, Vuudsh!" Guillermo screamed as he darted behind another hover vehicle.

Guillermo looked back down the street to see Vuudsh emerge from behind the hover truck, but just as he cocked his arm back to throw he was hit with a blast from the beetle tank and fell to the pavement. A heavy plasma bolt then pounded the truck, reducing it in one shot to a flaming mass of scrap metal.

Guillermo's heart nearly exploded from his chest as he rose from his position behind the hover vehicle and ran screaming at the tank, his plasma rifles unloading and bouncing harmlessly from its heavy armor. He approached it from behind and began kicking at one of its legs, shouting profanities, his teeth grinding with the effort.

The bug soldiers turned, cocking their heads to the side.

The tank began to turn, its heavy guns searching for the annoyance, and Guillermo now realized the error of his hasty attack. As it turned, he happened to notice a limping Aldrassan emerge from behind the burning hulk of the hover truck. It was Fuudqis, his fist holding the thermoplast aloft, and he was approaching the tank slowly. Guillermo spun to see that the bug soldiers were beginning to skirt the flaming hover car and take up flanking positions along the sides of the street.

"Heeeyy!" Guillermo screamed, kicking one of the hard legs of the tank. "Come get me, you ugly bug!"

The tank continued to turn toward him, its guns looking for something to destroy. Just as Fuudqis tossed the thermoplast Guillermo stumbled across the street to a door, blasting through it with a plasma bolt to make his escape.

The thermoplast shook the ground and shards of the tank penetrated the walls of the buildings around it. Guillermo ran back to the doorway and peered out to see the tank on its side, two of its legs still attached, and in the distance lay poor Vuudsh, his arms and legs splayed out in odd directions. To Guillermo's left the bug soldiers were beginning to regroup, and he looked beyond them at the shield that was still shimmering, a sign that it was still in full effect.

Taking in a deep breath, he ran across the street toward the blasted hole which used to be a doorway, bounding over hunks of twisted metal and flames and feeling the searing heat of plasma blasts that shot past his head. He dropped his rifles and grabbed Fuudqis by the arms, the Aldrassan's face badly burned, and dragged him to the alleyway. He ignored Fuudqis's feeble groan and ran back to do the same for Vuudsh, but the second Aldrassan was unresponsive. He shot across the street, grabbed up his plasma rifles, and returned to the first Aldrassan.

"The bugs are coming this way," he panted. "Can you move?"

Fuudqis stood slack, holding his side, his right cheek and eye a crust of blackened skin.

"I will manage," he wheezed.

"Get your butt inside the building. I'll see what I can do about the soldiers."

Fuudqis only nodded before running from the alley to an open doorway, trying to follow after the Gyaanik and the Nerds.

Guillermo, now alone, peered around the corner.

Several bug soldiers were filing down the street toward him, their plasma rifles pointed at the ground, their bodies low and crouching in rigid formations of tactical movement. However, the shimmering mirage that was the shield was no more, and he could clearly see the power station beyond.

With a mad shout of celebration, Guillermo began firing around the corner at the oncoming bug soldiers, and they took up defensive positions behind the remaining hover vehicles. They were cycling forward, severely outnumbering their lone Terran attacker. Guillermo stayed as long as he could, taking down several of the bug soldiers, but when they came too close he darted into the building after his Aldrassan comrades.

The screech of Ontoccan fighter craft could soon be heard, followed by the echoing boom of the destruction of the power plant.

CHAPTER 26

The bug soldiers followed Guillermo into the building, but Gyaanik, Fuudqis and the Nerds were waiting on them. The doorway was a choke point that allowed Guillermo and the Aldrassans to fell many of them.

Gyaanik touched a finger to his tiny ear, listening to a communication broadcast.

"They are detonating the pheromonal bomb," he said. "This may become worse."

Guillermo did not have time to argue, but dropped another bug soldier who had been apparently elected as cannon fodder. Soon the bug was followed by another, and another, but then no more soldiers piled through. He heard the distant blasts of plasma rifles and the concussive echo of bombs, but otherwise silence.

"I guess it worked," Guillermo said with a slight chuckle.

"Yes," clicked Nerd 1. "I can sense it in the air. It is unnerving."

After some deliberation, Guillermo and his squad determined that they would emerge from the building.

Falling into a tactical formation, they crept to the edge
of the doorway and peered out to see several bug
soldiers standing in the alleyway. When the bugs saw
Guillermo they only stared, their guns held in one hand,
pointed at the ground. One of the bugs nearest
Guillermo clicked his mandibles together.

"Why am I here?" he asked.

Guillermo's squad, one by one, stepped out into
the alley. After some time, Nerd 2 informed Guillermo
that these soldiers did not know that they were soldiers.
The ones that he could communicate with were
unaware that they were in a war at all. It was as if they
had been controlled by someone else.

He thought back to the skirmish in the forest,
how the bugs all spoke in unison. Somehow the Queen
was controlling her entire army with her mind, all of
them a thrall to her will.

He moved through the crowd of confused bug
soldiers, each of them standing in the alley as if they
had lost their will to move, their guns resting at their
sides. A thunderous noise was heard just then and a
rushing wind blew detritus around the alley as an
Ontoccan transport ship landed in the street. A ramp
dropped to the pavement and Zuraal emerged, his

overlarge pistol drawn. When he saw the state of the bug soldiers he holstered it and then jogged over to Guillermo.

"Victory's agent has smiled on us," he said. "Mitsuki is in safe arms at last. The doctor is en route to healing spring with her."

Guillermo looked over his shoulder at the mass of bug soldiers who were beginning to mill around aimlessly in the alley.

"What of them?" he asked. "It seems that they have no knowledge that they were in a war."

"We must hasten the reunion with your mate, Terran," said Zuraal with a toothy smile. Smiles on Guajiin always gave Guillermo the creeps. "She awaits you at the healing spring."

"You mean the hospital," he said. "Well, let's get there."

CHAPTER 27

Mitsuki lay in a stasis chamber after her treatment at the hospital. The doctors were able to remove the shard of metal from near her heart without complications, and now the healing chemical mist flowed over her, restoring her strength. The process took a matter of hours but when Guillermo arrived at the hospital all he could see was a crowd of Aldrassan nurses and other medical personnel surrounding her pod.

He approached the stasis chamber, a pill shaped pod, and placed his bionic hand on the bedrail, startling himself with the strange scratching sound it made. His attempt to process the day had left him dazed.

Her gown hid most of her injuries, and the swelling and bruising was gone from her face. He watched her sleep peacefully, his heart rising in tempo as his eyes traced the aquiline features of her delicate nose and chin. The medical personnel finished their various tasks and began filing out of the room until finally Guillermo stood alone by her bedside, the sound of their breathing and the whirring of medical equipment a soft drone.

"Mitsuki," he said, his voice a soft whisper. "You look great."

Her eyes flicked open and her gaze fell on him, her mouth a soft rosebud.

"Thanks," she said, her voice cracking. "I see you're still alive."

He chuckled a bit.

"Yeah," he said. "I'm hard to kill. Like a crulling cockroach. What do you say you and I blow this place and get some real food."

She only smiled, something that seemed to cause her pain. Her eyes squinted together and Guillermo reached out and touched her shoulder.

"It's…it's ok, Guillermo," she said. "Just a little strange. I thought I was dead for sure."

"Great to have you back."

There was a noise behind him and Guillermo turned to see Zuraal and Juuprish enter the room. Zuraal gave the normal greeting, standing a distance away, but Juuprish scurried forward and began to check the machines surrounding Mitsuki's bed. The Aldrassan hissed a few times, adjusting the dials and holographic read-outs. He uttered a soft growl and flicked a glance at Guillermo periodically.

"Something wrong?" asked Guillermo.

"Nothing of your concern," snapped Juuprish. "Her current condition is troubling, but I am sure she will make a full recovery."

"What do you mean, troubling?" Guillermo asked, his face drawn.

"Nothing, nothing…she is fine. Just fine."

Guillermo squinted his eyes at Juuprish.

"You're not telling me something, Juuprish. I think I've earned the right to know what that is."

The Aldrassan laughed.

"Earned? What have you earned? Nothing. You helped us destroy the power plant, a task that we could have accomplished on our own. You are not required for our success."

Zuraal fidgeted a bit, folded both sets of arms.

"Look," Guillermo said, gritting his teeth. "Say what you want about me. This was a means to an end is all. Mitsuki has the care she needs, you got your city back, so why don't you step off and cut me some *crulling slack*!"

Zuraal stomped across the floor and stood between them.

"Truce," he boomed, one hand instinctively on his

revolver. "Your alliance is in blood, Guillermo. Stay your dueling challenge."

All was silent for a moment save for the whirr of the medical devices.

"As promised," Guillermo said, his hands wringing the bedrail. "I get a fast ship to find my friend."

"You shall have it," Juuprish said coldly. "And you will take the female with you."

The door swooshed open just then and a bug wearing Ontoccan black scurried into the room.

"It is urgent that we convene with Yalrykk, Zuraal," he said, his mandibles clicking frantically. "The Queen's forces have regrouped at the tech research facility and have sent us an ultimatum."

"We must act," Juuprish said. "We cannot lose the tech facility. It holds the key to reclaiming Ontocca."

The bug produced a small holographic communicator and swiped a claw-like hand over it. A bluish transparent image emerged.

A bug appeared, her face familiar to Guillermo, but he had to move closer to be sure.

"The message is repeating," said the bug,

thumbing the holo into motion. "I will play it for you."

Dervish, the unmistakable scar on her left cheek from a bounty hunter's blade clearly visible, began to utter the clicking and hissing that constituted Terran speech.

"The sensory bomb you released was effective against the drones," she said. "But not against my royal guard. We have taken the tech facility and will destroy it unless you bring us the Terrans immediately. That is all."

The image faded, then winked out with a final bright flash.

"Holy chert, that was Dervish!" Guillermo exclaimed. "She's been brainwashed just like all the rest of them."

Juuprish stroked his pointy chin.

"It is something ancient that controls them... something I thought was only a myth."

"What do you mean?" Guillermo asked.

"The bugs, in ancient times, were a star-faring culture. They had conquered all worlds of the Five Rims much as your kind did in more recent history. It was believed that the Queen could make thralls of her subjects using some type of crown. They ruled the Five

Rims for centuries until a religious order arose that changed their culture entirely, and they reverted back to a simpler and less technological way of life, giving up their empire. Perhaps if they had not done so your kind would have been defeated when you appeared in our realm so long ago, and we would probably not be at war right now."

"Or you'd be thrall to the Queen," Guillermo countered. "You ever think about that?"

Guillermo stepped around the bed, past Zuraal, and then moved into Juuprish's personal space, something he knew Aldrassans hated.

"Look, pal. I don't give an Ukmoraad's fart about the past or what could have been."

"Ukmoraad's fart," Zuraal chuckled. Guillermo shot him a sidelong glance, then continued, pressing a metallic finger into Juuprish's chest.

"All I care about is getting Dervish back. Now if that means joining an assault force to attack the tech facility, then so be it. But I'm done being racially blamed for the actions of my people. Yeah we conquered you, yeah we enslaved you, and yeah we took a huge steaming dump on your culture, but I just want to move on. Do you think you can help me out with that?"

The Aldrassan didn't say a word, only tightened his lips, nodded, and then strode out of the room leaving a silence that even seemed to deafen the medical devices.

"Heart is broken, Guillermo," said Zuraal finally. "His order forbids eating peace feast with you."

"Well," Guillermo said coldly. "Maybe he ought to get a better religion."

Mitsuki opened her eyes.

"What should I do?" she asked, her voice weak. "I could help."

Guillermo reached out a hand and stroked her hair. It was remarkably soft against his skin.

"You rest," he said. "We got this."

She nodded and closed her eyes, and Guillermo put a hand on Zuraal's shoulder, pulling him over away from the bed and against the far wall.

"What's the plan, Zuraal?"

"In the corral we have detained the enemy," he said. "Their minds cannot remember-draw their purpose, and they are no longer itching for the fight."

"So the main forces that were affected by the bomb are of no use to the Queen anymore. Dervish, or the Queen or whatever, is claiming that the pheromonal bomb won't work on her royal guard. They are a lot tougher than the normal drones, trust me."

"What are you drawing?"

"I'm *drawing* that we send everything we've got at the tech facility," said Guillermo. "She's expecting you guys to just hand us over since she thinks you don't care about us that much anyway, right?"

"But you are blood-brother born, Guillermo."

"Yeah," Guillermo laughed. "Pretend I'm not. Just go with me on this."

CHAPTER 28

The city was eerily silent, yet squirming with the activity of a hive, each invader an extension of the will of one mind.

She no longer felt the call of her own desires, her own ideas, but she did feel the pull of the One flooding her mind with a singular task: guard. It was not a complete over-riding of thought, but a suggestive force of will that guided her and rewarded her compliance with endorphins. However, any resistance shot an explosive kick to her pain center. Her mind was therefore over-written with the desires of the One, a powerful urge to only do what was commanded, even if that command was singular and extremely basic. She no longer thought about her own will, for now work never ended, her senses focused on the safety of the tech facility. She ignored the worker drones who attended it night and day, their bodies moving sluggishly after a two day shift without rest.

Guard. Secure. Obey.

She did not really understand the purpose of the tech facility, only that it was to be guarded, to be protected with her life, and somehow the control was too overwhelming to think of anything else but the mission. She had given up fighting against the hot lava flow that was the will of the One.

The One had convinced her that the Terrans were to be hated.

At once she was on edge.

Suddenly her senses felt a hot wind and a scent that commingled with it. It was not the terrible pheromonal bomb for which every ounce of control had to be focused to resist, but something familiar and forbidden to discuss. The scent filled her advanced olfactory nerves, overpowering her conditioning, but did not prevent her from acting according to command as she flicked her wrist to prepare her weapon, a long shaft with an electrified blade at the end, crackling with energy.

She could see them, but they could not see her.

The Ontoccans were trying to move with stealth, even using the cover of the jungle and a locally grown salve to mask their scent. She was not fooled, would not fail in her mission by pain of death. She clung to the black metallic ceiling of the facility like a predatory spider waiting for its prey, her compatriots also at the ready, their silent pheromonal communication on the soft warm breeze.

She let the enemy move in, let them sneak closely to the blind and unwary workers with knives extended, and she had been instructed allow their sacrificial deaths, her fellow bug drones only following the will of the One. She did not think of victory, of cherishing the thrill of the hunt as she would have in her past life. She was focused on the task at hand, of fulfilling the will of the One.

Slowly, in unison, the Royal Guard descended on small filament lines attached to their thorax harnesses. Noiselessly they fell upon the Ontoccans and she saw the one that emitted the familiar scent, a special prize, and now the One took more active control, focusing all attention on that being. He was a Terran, his plasma rifle held in tense hands, his black hair a mop dripping with sweat. She was ready to pounce on him, and any conflict she had with the One melted away in a fire of painful control.

The Terran turned to look at her, his face an unreadable blob, as she had always had difficulty understanding Terran emotional cues. He did not raise his rifle, but his lips uttered something familiar. A name. Before she brought the glaive down he parried it with his metal arm just inches from his neck.

"Dervish! What the..." was all he managed to say as she attacked him.

She moved quickly, her glaive spinning and slashing with expert precision as she beat the Terran back into a corner, his lips moving, highlighted by the sudden blue light of plasma fire as he tried to get her to read his lips, to remember her oath to protect him from harm.

"Dervish!" he screamed, his metallic arm catching the electro-glaive again, straining to hold it as the blue energy danced down the shaft to crackle across his arm. He jerked his head to the side to avoid the stinging blast. "You've got to stop! You've got to remember! What the crull happened to you?"

She did not listen, the drone of the voice of the One in her mind drowning out any sense of loyalty or understanding, her mind focused on the will of her Queen who controlled all of her subjects with the power of the C'Tuul'U'Hindra.

Her forces moved in, reinforced by several hundred who had lain in wait within tunnels burrowed deep beneath the foundation, down where the secret and ancient reactor could warm them. And now they flooded out of these burrows, overwhelming the enemy and being ordered not to chase those who fled. The real prize was the Terran, and they were instructed not to harm but to capture.

The Terran did not come easily, for he somehow managed to pull the electro-glaive from Dervish's grasp and attack several nearby soldiers before running toward the outer perimeter of the courtyard where he had first entered. He hesitated, fought off some more of the hive, then looked at her with his strangely liquid eyes before attempting to run. He could not, however, because his legs were snared in the electro-netting, and then he was down, covered in the hive.

She could then feel the pride of the One as she bathed them in her approval, a pleasurable response that forced her to her knees. They had completed their assigned task, the chemical pleasure of reward flooding their brains. They had captured the Terran.

CHAPTER 29

Guillermo felt searing pain, a hot iron sting that drove deep into his shoulder and knee joints like a molten knife. He tried to get his bearings, but the inky black darkness enfolded him in an embrace he was hopeless to escape. Something had wrapped itself around his limbs and was holding him tight, squeezing and cutting off the circulation to his right hand and his feet.

As the light painfully flooded his optic nerves, a blinding experience that caused him to blink furiously, he could feel the choker vines that held him in place. He had been stretched out as if he were on a medieval rack, and before him stood the unmistakable shape of Dervish.

She took two steps forward, her hands clasped behind her back.

"Ah, you are awake," she said, her mandibles clicking and purring. "At last you can see the truth of the Ontoccan Hegemony and realize the futility of your alliance with them."

"What the crull, Dervish," Guillermo groaned. "What did they do to you?"

"Your name for this guard is amusing," said Dervish, referring to herself. "At times I wish your kind could experience the true sense of our experience, the scent of reality. I am afraid you would find it too overwhelming to comprehend."

Guillermo felt a sadness that was nearly unbearable. He stared at Dervish for some time before responding to her, knowing now that his friend of two years was now a slave to the mind of the Queen.

His desperation caused his despair to suddenly boil over into anger.

"Get on with it, v'oshtu," Guillermo growled as he squirmed in his bonds. "I have a dental appointment later...wouldn't want to miss it."

"Terran humor. Fascinating. Your kind is typical. Even when you were torturing our kind and all the other Five Rims races during your regime you did not understand how small you were. Those days are over, however, and I will make sure Terrans never rise to power again."

Dervish turned then, and with a flick of her wrist the vine released him, dropping him to the floor. He rose to all fours and then to his feet. Several plasma rifles whirred to life, a high-pitched signature whine, and Guillermo noticed a dozen or so bug soldiers standing around the edges of the hazy chamber.

"Follow this royal guard," Dervish said, referring to herself again as she walked toward an oval door that opened automatically. "She will enlighten you to the lies of the Ontoccans."

For lack of a better plan, Guillermo followed as ordered, his ankle now only sore from his injury in the mine. Dervish led him along a hallway that ended rather abruptly at a heavy round door. A security panel emerged from the wall through a slot and Dervish pressed a few keys on the keypad.

"Behold your folly," said Dervish as the thick metal door irised open. Beyond, in a darkened cavernous room, ambient light revealed what looked like rows and rows of crates.

"Your people have been betrayed," she said, her arms spread wide.

The first thing that struck Guillermo's senses was the horrible odor, like that of ripened sewage or compost, and as the lights slowly pushed back the darkness he could see that the long row of of crates was actually one large, slightly rusted and disused cage containing about a twenty or so Terrans. Each shambling Terran wore a simple tattered tunic, their long unkempt hair wild and tangled in places due to neglect. The men, all of them with long, matted beards stood at the bars and growled at Dervish and Guillermo as the two passed along. Guillermo was suddenly startled by a woman who hissed at him before clutching at her small filthy child and dragging it away into the shadows.

"What is this?" Guillermo muttered, his voice cracking.

"It is the truth," Dervish replied. "The Ontoccan secret to unlocking the ancient Terran technology. It requires a live Terran, activated by their DNA. The Ontoccans have been keeping this stock of Terrans alive for that purpose, keeping it secret from everyone but my spies. When I found out I knew that this was the way to break their hold over us, to break the unholy hegemony forever."

"What do you plan to —"

"Do?" said Dervish, cutting him off. "We plan to exterminate these vermin, of course."

Guillermo sank to his knees, tears clouding his eyes.

"By the maker, what do you want?" he cried.

"Don't do this!"

"It is why your Ontoccan friends wished to take back this satellite city rather than the capitol. And once we exterminate this breeding stock, the Ontoccan dominance over technology in the Five Rims will be broken."

Guillermo fell forward, his body in a crawling position as he stared at the filthy floor, its surface littered with bits of straw and grime. He spat a glistening wad of spit before rising to his feet and charging Dervish. She simply side-stepped him, and in seconds Guillermo was overwhelmed by armored bug soldiers who dragged him to the ground.

He was rolled over onto his back and held in place by iron hands as he grit his teeth and stared at the lights far above him, hissing and moaning. Soon, however, Dervish was towering over him, in her hand a small pistol with a barbed tip. She casually pointed it at his chest, then powered up the stunner.

"Your prize is ready, my Queen," said Dervish.

She did not fire, however, as a deafening thump was heard from somewhere outside the room. The bug soldiers began to move, each of them twitching with activity as they fanned out and began to take up defensive positions around the entrance. One of the bug soldiers was suddenly vaporized as a large hole blew open to the right of the door and Dervish shrank back, stealing a plasma rifle from one of her soldiers.

"Don't do this!" Guillermo said. "I'll bet that's the Ontoccans. If you'll fight the Queen's control and surrender I'm sure they'll go easy on you. Come on, Dervish, you have to fight it!"

"These Terrans are useless," she said, her hands gripping the rifle tightly. "The Ontoccans lobotomize them when they are born. They are nothing but cattle."

She switched the gun over to automatic and opened fire on the mass of Terrans, all of them futilely covering their heads and crouching to the litter-strewn floor. Guillermo screamed, leaping from the ground and sprinting toward her, his eyes on fire with rage. He was able to grasp the weapon, but not before Dervish had executed the feral Terrans, their bodies lying in heaps beyond the rusty bars.

She wrenched the rifle away from him as the doors to the chamber burst open and Zuraal tumbled through, crushing two of the bug soldiers to the floor with his mighty arms.

"Guillermo!" shouted the Guajiin, who was

followed through the breach by a cadre of Ontoccan regulars. "Are you safe in mother's arms?"

Before he could respond, Guillermo was thrown to the grimy floor by Dervish who then leaped to the top of the cage with barely a sound. She scurried up the wall and out a vent high above the floor, dropping the plasma rifle which clattered near Guillermo's feet. He picked it up, and unloaded on the vent before roaring and then dispatching the remaining bug soldiers.

Soon they stood in silence, the only sound Guillermo's sobs.

"Uncover the nest, we did," Zuraal offered, and then he stopped in mid sentence, staring at the twenty or so dead Terrans in the cage.

One giant hand went to the top of his bald head and scratched.

"U'draad m'huulagraab," said the Guajiin, his native tongue rolling the "r"'s.

Some Guajiin phrasings defied translation. This was true of this particular phrase, but conveyed an emotion of utter despair.

Guillermo, the plasma rifle crashing to the floor, pushed his way past the Ontoccan soldiers, fighting through their ranks violently.

He had to get some air.

CHAPTER 30

Zuraal and the Ontoccan soldiers stood in silence for some time, staring at the heaps of dead Terrans lying in the rusted cage. One of the Aldrassan soldiers approached the bars, placed one six-fingered hand on the metal and bowed his head. Zuraal turned to his lieutenant, a deep frown forming on his tusked face, and gave the order to begin removing the bodies to the courtyard outside.

"Yalrykk must know of this," he said. "The sore must be lanced with a clean dagger. Shamed am I."

There was a noise without and Guillermo bolted back into the room. He shoved Zuraal with both hands, nearly toppling the three-meter tall Guajiin.

"What the crull is this?" he screamed. "Dervish said you Ontoccans used these Terrans as cattle to unlock the DNA triggers on Terran tech!"

Zuraal backed away, all four of his arms raised in a defensive posture.

"I do not remember-draw this place, Guillermo," he said, his voice wavering, his small black eyes watery. "It is a prey-trail gone cold. Much shame had visited my clan!"

Guillermo looked around at the other Ontoccan soldiers, their faces all blank as far as he could read of their alien physiology, but their body language was all the same: shock.

"Get Juuprish in here!" Guillermo shouted. "That v'oshtu is going to —"

"That v'oshtu as you are so fond of saying," said Juuprish from the broken doorway. "Is asking that you keep your voice down."

Guillermo pushed past Zuraal and rushed at the Aldrassan, but Juuprish was quick, dodging to the side and slipping around behind him, placing him in an immobilizing hold.

"Keep calm," said Juuprish, his breathing normal, not winded at all. "I will explain everything to you when you calm down."

"I'll calm down when you monsters are all dead, Juuprish," Guillermo croaked, the Aldrassan's thin forearm against his throat.

Guillermo grabbed the Aldrassan's elbow with his metal hand and squeezed, the servos in the wrist whining, and the Aldrassan squealed as the bones were crushed to powder. Guillermo then held the arm tightly, feeling the bits of bone grind together as he stomped down along the Aldrassan's shin with the edge of his boot, obliterating Juuprish's naked foot.

Suddenly Guillermo felt large hands grab his arms and hoist him above the floor, but he struggled against them, his teeth gnashing, his eyes wild. It was of little use, as the second set of arms wrapped around his waist and held him snug, not enough to cut off his breathing, but just enough to cause him to begin to calm down.

"Listen to his words, Juuprish," came Zuraal's basso voice from behind Guillermo's ear. "A truth-tale must be spun now. This place is an unholy thing, a sabbat-hulaar. You have dishonored the brood with its unveiling and visited shame upon our clan."

Suddenly all the other Ontoccans joined in, chastising Juuprish, demanding answers. Questions, hard questions, were being asked of him, but he could only sink to the floor in pain and whimper, holding his broken elbow and scooting away from them.

He continued to slide away toward the door, but then Yalrykk, the old Aldrassan elder, entered the doorway and leaned against the frame. Yalrykk hung his head and stared at Juuprish, and when the injured Aldrassan tried to speak to him he was silenced with a series of clicks and guttural howls of Aldrassan warnings.

Yalrykk, his face ashen, his shoulders slumping, then looked at Guillermo, his dark eyes two reflective orbs.

"This was what we did not want you to know," said Yalrykk, his voice cracking. "It was our only way to hold sway over the hegemony, to control the technology that you Terrans left behind. Only a few of us knew of this place, and we are ashamed that you have found it in this way. We never intended—"

Guillermo was released then, but before he could reach for Yalrykk, before he could exact revenge, a loud explosion nearly deafened him as a hole blew through Yalrykk's chest and out the other side. Several soldiers gasped and muttered, and Guillermo turned to see the smoking barrel of Zuraal's ancestral gun before he aimed it at Juuprish and pulled the trigger a second time.

Guillermo then heard the mingling languages of the Five Rim races as each Ontoccan soldier reacted to the deaths of their leaders, and Zuraal holstered his revolver slowly, the barrel still smoking.

He held up all four hands and twisted his heavy

waist as he addressed his army.

"Justice swift is Ontoccan way," he shouted. "May we all unify under our common plight as it is said and always shall be said."

He heard the others repeat a phrase back to him as the room settled.

As slaves we were unified. As free beings we will forever be so.

As if on cue, the Ontoccans began opening the cage to gently carry the dead Terrans out of the building. Zuraal placed a hand on Guillermo's shoulder.

"My charge. Heroes on the high burning altar these of your family shall be honored. Shame's shadow follows us on our new journey."

Guillermo was soon surrounded by the Ontoccan soldiers who each placed a gentle hand on his back and shoulders, anywhere they could touch him, and he heard the Fraaz in their number begin a death howl that was common to their kind, a howl of mourning.

Over the next hour they carefully removed the bodies of the Terrans from their cage, each one filthy and grimy, the pock-marked corpses of men, women and three children. The bodies were brought out of the

facility and laid in the courtyard outside the front
entrance of the tech facility for all Ontoccans to see.
Many of them, still finding their way to the facility after
nearly a week in exile, murmured and whispered to
each other, their faces aghast at the sight of the dead
Terrans.

CHAPTER 31

Mitsuki had graduated to a hospital bed, and that was a plus, but Guillermo sat on a high metal stool nearby, a brooding carrion bird contemplating revenge. Mitsuki awoke, her brown eyes fluttering open, and she rubbed them with dainty hands before noticing Guillermo and taking in a sharp breath.

"Talk to me," she said, her eyes studying him.

He sat in silence, his metallic finger tapping on the stool methodically, a calculating clock that kept time with his rage.

"Guillermo?" she asked, sitting up slightly, propping herself up on her elbows. Only one tube ran to her forearm, a far cry from the multitude of devices plugged into her skin over the past few days.

"They kept us as pets, Mitsuki," Guillermo finally growled. "Crulling pets. Seems they needed Terran DNA to reverse engineer the security protocols on the Terran tech, develop vaccines, test new drugs. They couldn't have just crulling *asked* for our help with it. No! They had to keep us in a pen like animals and lobotomize us."

"Guillermo? What are you talking about?"

He dropped from the stool to the floor and began pacing. Picked up the stool. Tossed it to the wall with a clatter.

"You feeling better?" he asked, his voice a staccato. "Think you can travel?"

"Um," Mitsuki replied softly, her lips pursing. "Not sure what you mean…"

"I'm saying we get the crull out of here…now… today. Can't stay here…I want to just leave, to find Dervish, to kill that crulling Queen."

The door to the room swooshed open, the portal irising, and Zuraal stood in the hall outside. He hesitated, then stepped into the room, and Guillermo spun to face him.

"Whatever you got to say can't be that important, Guajiin," Guillermo roared, pointing one accusatory finger. "You Ontoccans have been keeping some kind of…lab…experiment…running here without letting the other Terrans know about it?"

Zuraal stood quietly, all four arms at his sides, and then let out a heavy breath.

"In the crypt lay the rusted old trap," Zuraal said, his voice slightly hoarse. "Listening to the music of the lure, was I…was all the others. Only the leaders knew."

"Chert on that!" Guillermo shouted, his finger stabbing the air. "I'll believe nothing else you say to me, that any of you Five Rims species say to me. I crulling *helped* your resistance against the bugs, Zuraal. I lost valuable chids on most of the runs I made... through bug infested space, with crulling bounty hunters everywhere. And all the while you're...you're keeping twenty or so pet Terrans? For what? Experimentation? Those people were living like animals!"

"Broken is the treaty of the genocidal war, Guillermo," Zuraal countered. "Heart of ancestors weeps the blood of the young...and we on our knees bow before the mercy of the duel-winner."

"Spare me your metaphorical apology, Zuraal," Guillermo growled. "My heart is black, if that means anything to you. It's a charred chunk of hardened durasteel."

Mitsuki cleared her throat and Guillermo could feel her hand on his back.

"Zuraal has shown you nothing but kindness, Guillermo...the both of us," she said.

He turned to see her standing beside him,

holding on to the tube running into her arm. Those eyes of hers did their best to cool the fire, but it only fired the steam.

"You didn't see it," Guillermo whispered.

The door irised open again, and this time half of Guillermo's former strike team entered. Gyaanik and Fuudqis displayed the same serious expressions they showed in the field only twelve hours ago.

"Commander," said Gyaanik, nearly out of breath. "We have come to retrieve you, sir. The Queen has launched all forces in the surrounding cities to crush our victory. We must prepare for the worst."

"We will answer the call of the hunt," boomed Zuraal. "But first we must smooth the feathers of the aal'drak."

The two Aldrassans each folded their hands before them and bowed their heads in one quick jerk.

"Our leaders have dishonored us," said Vuudsh, who was the youngest of two commandos. "It is a dishonor for which we are unable to make amends, Terran. Your service to our world has been beyond the call of —"

"Save your breath, Vuudsh," Guillermo said, and felt Mitsuki squeeze his arm, but he pulled away. "You have a chert-load of answers to give about what was really going on here."

Gyaanik stepped forward, shirking custom, invading Guillermo's personal space and standing close enough so that Guillermo could see the Aldrassan's shark-like teeth.

"Let it be known, Terran," he said, his voice low. "We will find justice for your kind. Your ancestors helped us free ourselves from the Phaedran Empire, and even though we are often annoyed by your crude customs we are at our core forever grateful for the kindness of that brief union of our peoples. The Terran resistance will not be forgotten, but I am afraid there will always be a remnant of the Five Rims races who believe that your kind are genetically prone to the need to dominate others. Our leaders have deceived us as well. Please understand."

Guillermo paused, the corner of his mouth twisting slightly and his eyes narrowing.

"Sure," he said. "But what should we do about the here and now? I, for one, am done with helping your rebellion, and you Five Rims stiffs can just tear each other apart for all I care. Mitsuki?"

He turned to look at her, and she plopped down

on the bed in response.

"You think you can travel?" he asked.

"You're not thinking of leaving right now, are you?" she said, and the others began to mutter to themselves.

"Chert yes," he said. "Just as soon as we can get to a ship."

The two Aldrassans tried to move toward Guillermo, their arms out but Zuraal held them back with one large arm. With the another he reached for Guillermo, but then dropped it to his side. The Guajiin then let out a long sigh, hanging his head.

"We are honor bound to your request," Zuraal said finally. "Name your mount, Terran."

"You are not considering giving him a ship, Commander?" Gyaanik protested, his mouth wide. "We need all available craft to repel the bugs and take back our planet!"

"It is a debt paid in blood," growled Zuraal, turning to look down at the two commandos. "Our ancestors demand our compliance."

It was agreed then, and without words Guillermo and Mitsuki prepared to leave.

After Mitsuki disappeared into a side room to

gingerly change into a plain black Ontoccan uniform, the two Terrans exited the hospital room leaving Zuraal and the Aldrassans standing in silence.

After a few moments, Zuraal turned to his subordinates, his four arms hanging limp at his sides, and then the youngest Aldrassan shouted something in his own tongue, something vile.

"Why," Vuudsh hissed. "Of all the Terrans left in the Five Rims, did the last one have to be such a c'huu'drahiin?"

And then the bombs began to drop.

CHAPTER 32

"Wait! Wait!....*Wait!*" Mitsuki screamed as she pulled away from Guillermo.

He had been dragging her along behind him, hell-bent on getting to a shuttle and leaving this planet behind. They stood beneath a canopy just outside the hospital, and the sound of plasma bombs and enemy fighters grew in intensity by the minute. Guillermo seemed to ignore them, but it made Mitsuki's eyelids flutter with each concussive blast.

He marched forward without her, then turned back and reached out his hand.

"What," he shouted.

"We can't just leave them," she exclaimed. "They need your help…and they healed me, so that has to count for something."

"Mitsuki, they lied to us…all of it was a lie! They were using our people as lab mice…that's all we are to them. You didn't see the bodies!"

She folded her arms, wincing through the soreness.

"Our people were brutal to them, Guillermo. If the Queen takes this planet she will control the Five

Rims. Only their leadership knew about the lab...not Zuraal...not our friends."

He stood with his arms at his sides, his fingers twitching. His brow furrowed and he bared his teeth.

"You and I are all that's left, Mitsuki," he bellowed. "I think you might want to consider our own skins. This planet is lost anyway, and if you'll look around you'll realize it."

The bombs were getting closer and black smoke began to invade the tarmac where two space-worthy shuttles sat idle. Several Ontoccans scurried around, and some of them were pushing past them, trying to find shelter in the underground floors of the hospital. The two Terrans stood silent in the middle of the increasing flow of Ontoccans, two immovable stones in the middle of a rushing stream.

Finally she spoke, a single tear rolling down her cheek.

"For the last man in the universe you sure are a horrible example of humanity, Guillermo," she said, her lip quivering. "If you leave, if we leave, then we prove to them that Terrans are who they think we are...selfish and impulsive...irredeemable. We have to go back and see what we can do."

He stood for a moment, his mouth set, and then he reached for her.

"Come with me, then," he said. "I'm no good on the ground anyway. If we can get to a gunship I think we can do the most damage."

She pushed past him, not taking his hand, her eyes scanning the tarmac outside the hospital as she trotted beside him.

"I don't see a gunship, Guillermo," she said. "All I can see are these useless triage shuttles. No weapons on board."

The throng of various races were becoming hard to push against, their numbers growing as they began to crowd the door to the hospital looking for a safe haven from the bombs. An Ontoccan fighter zipped low overhead causing a wave of screams as it took several blasts from a pursuing bug fighter and then crashed into the hospital, a fireball exploding outward that scattered debris into the mob. Guillermo and Mitsuki began to run, pushing through the crowd toward a nearby temporary landing strip where a gunship sat unused, a fuel line plugged into the fuselage.

"There!" Mitsuki shouted. "Right over there!"

Guillermo didn't respond, pushing through the crowd to the gunship with Mitsuki hot on his heels. In a few moments they reached it, and an Aldrassan pilot, wearing an oblong helmet and black flight suit, stared at them as they rushed past him up the landing ramp. Mitsuki stopped briefly to shrug as they boarded, and the pilot shrugged as well, then ran to a nearby fighter right before he and the craft were vaporized by a well-aimed bomb.

Mitsuki and Guillermo fired up the engines on the gunship and lifted off, the repulsers emitting a soft blue glow as the afterburners kicked in, rocketing them toward a buzzing hive of fighters. The sleek design of the heavy armored gunship dwarfed many of the enemy fighters, but hanging in the sky, dropping yellowish flares of light on the city that decimated structures and lives, were three bug dreadnaughts bristling with hundreds of guns.

Neither Terran spoke as they assumed their roles on board, Mitsuki manning the rear guns as Guillermo piloted the ship deep into the enemy formation. The shields flared blue as the first volley of plasma bolts began to strike them. He continued on, pushing the throttle further and adjusting all remaining power to

the forward shields. Mitsuki tried her best to keep the
fighters that fell in behind them from succeeding at
their mission.

He could hear her from the gunnery position at
the rear of the gunship as she shouted and screamed,
the signature pump-pump-pump of the massive plasma
cannon raining death on anyone that dared follow
them. In all the madness Guillermo rarely fired,
sporadically pulling the trigger on his forward cannon,
doing so sparingly only when a rogue fighter attempted
to play an old game of "yard bird" with him. He
remained silent, focused, his eyes on the gap between
the dreadnaughts, and soon he began to see the blue
sky turn deep midnight and then black with tiny stars
sparkling everywhere, and they were out above the
atmosphere.

Mitsuki's steady voice came from aft.

"Guillermo, where are we going? They aren't
following us anymore."

He remained silent, pushing the gunship ever
forward, rocketing away from Ontocca and toward the
asteroid field that ringed the planet.

"Gonna hide out in that field, Mitsuki," he
responded finally, his eyes narrowing. "I think we can

make another run at them from in there…or at least keep them off of us."

This response did not satisfy her, and she appeared in the doorway to the cockpit, her eyes wide.

"You're running anyway!" she roared. "You are such a — "

"It's for the best!" he argued. "I didn't think you were going to see it my way so I told you a lie. It's what I'm good at. Surviving…and probably lying. We're the last of our kind, Mitsuki! You'd think you'd be a little more — "

He felt a hard blow against the back of his skull, saw stars, and then turned to face her, glaring.

"You know that old saying about being the last man on Terra?" she said. "Well, you just figure that one out."

She hit him again, this time on the back of the right shoulder, shouted something unintelligible, then ran to the back of the ship where suddenly he heard an access panel clatter to the floor.

"What are you doing?" he shouted, keeping his eye on the asteroids ahead.

They were getting ominously closer.

He heard something like the sound of insulated

cabling being pulled from the bulkhead, and then the lights began to flicker on the control panel and the sensor scope readout went dark.

"Mitsuki!" he screamed, slowing the ship slightly. "We're in the middle of a war here and you want to sabotage our—"

Something hit the hull, and it wasn't a plasma blast.

He pulled back on the stick and smacked the console with his fist. Just then Mitsuki emerged holding an oblong chunk of metal with several tubes jutting out of it from several angles.

"We won't be going anywhere without our graviton projector," she said coldly.

"How did you—?"

"Those Fraaz taught me a few things," she said with a grin. "I'm a quick study."

Guillermo remembered the brief "help" she had given to the Fraaz back in the cave base and growled.

"Put it back," he commanded.

Something else struck the hull, something bigger.

"No way," she said.

That smirk appeared again, but this time it wasn't inviting.

"I'll lock you in the hold and put it back myself. We're headed into an asteroid field, the shields route through the graviton projector, and unless you want to be pulverized by Ontocca's former moon then you'll do as you're told."

"I said no," and she threw the graviton emitter aft.

Guillermo, muttering profanities, spun and shot Mitsuki with a stunner.

She dropped to the deck.

"I really hated to do that," he said to her softly. "But you really left me no choice."

After a few moments of hasty repairs where Guillermo muttered more profanity and a few more asteroids barked the hull outside, he prepared the ship for a jump through a wormhole and had to rap on the console with his fist to get it to engage. Just before the final sequence spun up, his eyes widened as a chrome ball appeared in space just to starboard and a gargantuan craft emerged, a spheroid black ship covered with spines like that of a sea urchin, each crackling with what looked like yellow lightning.

The Queen had arrived.

He turned his eyes away, focusing on the control

panel with the countdown visible, and could see his own smaller wormhole forming in front of him, reflecting the star of a distant place far away from the Five Rims, a place he hoped would be safe from the Queen.

That was when his gunship rocked with the force of something enormous, too strong to be a stray asteroid. Even though he could see the Queen's ship in the distance, something was swallowing him up, casting him into a shadow of starless night.

He felt a jolt through his bones as every panel in his ship exploded in a shower of sparks and he fell helplessly to the deck next to Mitsuki.

CHAPTER 33

In his dream the island approached him again, a
glowing place of tall narrow trees and little sign of life,
devoid of buildings or farms or any other marring of the
landscape. He flew between narrow trees, their leaves
striking him across the face. Something was aglow in
the dense foliage, something that pulsated and grew
clearer as he approached it, and as he reached the
center of the island he saw a spiraling ladder, a glowing
crystalline ladder that he recognized as the building
code for all life, but specifically Terran life.

The strand of spiraling DNA coiled and pulsated,
shrinking smaller and smaller, moving toward him in
the gloom. He reached for it, felt it pass through his
fingers and sink into his hand.

Then something bit him.

He opened his eyes and found himself in a two
meter by two meter cage, the bars made of hexagons,
surrounding him in a honeycomb spherical ball. He
was suspended in mid-air by a gravitic stasis field and
apparently he had floated too close to the metallic
honeycomb and had been shocked awake by the energy
that flowed through the bars.

He looked around him, finding that the cage was
also suspended above the floor of the room he occupied,
floating in the center of this cube of a room, and that
only one doorway was visible. It was closed, split down
the middle with a magnetic seal. He had never seen

such an elaborate cell. He knew, however, that he had escaped from many other prisons before, and realized that his captor probably had checked that box.

"Hey!" he screamed, but the echo of his own voice was all that he could hear save the faint rumble that told him he was in space traveling at high speed.

Mitsuki.

He tried to move again, this time his body floating toward the energized hexagonal bars, and he halted his movements. He floated back toward the center, now suspended in mid-air. He felt around on his waist and found a gravitic belt fastened there. He pulled at it, realizing that it had been locked onto him and his attempt to move it only caused it to cinch up on his hips a little tighter and deliver a painful shock.

He grunted through his teeth.

A door whooshed open, and Duuzra crawled forward on his armored wings, the faceless helmet staring up at him.

"To struggle is to bring pain," he said, his voice modulated into a deep vibrato. "You should be proud. The Queen was generous enough to allow me to transport you to my planet. I will show you what your kind did to us before removing a little part of your brain to make you more compliant...like the rest."

"Let me out of here and we'll see what pain is all about you crulling cave worm."

Duuzra clung to the wall, scrambling along using his clawed feet and the strange digits at the bend of his wings. His armor whirred, aiding him as he moved, and when he reached the ceiling he hung from his feet and enveloped himself in his wings. Each web between his digits were covered in a flexible red armor sheeting. The helmeted head, a triangular shape with two metallic, pointed ears, turned to face Guillermo.

"Would you like to eat?" he asked. "I am sure you require sustenance. The nanites in your blood stream are probably tearing the rest of you apart in order to repair your injuries."

"I'll manage," Guillermo spat. "Where is Mitsuki?"

The bounty hunter cocked his head to the side.

"I will bring you some sustenance," Duuzra insisted, dropping to the floor and catching the air with his wide wings just before landing. "You will eat the sustenance or you will suffer pain."

The bounty hunter exited the door like some mechanical vermin, his wings making grating metal noises, leaving Guillermo to seethe and eventually scream epithets at the walls. After a time, Duuzra emerged from the door again and crawled to his perch on the ceiling.

"I am prepared to feed you. You will comply or you will suffer pain."

"I'm used to pain, vermin," Guillermo snarled. "Just shut your noise and let me enjoy it."

Something worse than electric shock suddenly coursed through Guillermo's body, and his screams echoed off of the walls of his prison, drowning out the low rumble of space travel and the soft chuckle of his captor.

"You will comply or you will suffer pain," Duuzra intoned calmly. "Strapped to your skin is a device taken from the Terran language-learning machines that the bugs were forced to use during the Phaedran Empire's occupation. It is a gift from the Queen. It is dialed in to the frequency of your pain receptors and is an efficient method for forcing compliance."

"You know what, Fraaz?" Guillermo chuckled through gritted teeth. "I'm glad the Terrans nuked your crulling planet. Every one of your kind is a cherty little vermin."

"You attempt to bait me," Duuzra droned. "You will not succeed. It is illogical for you to do so because the only alternative is pain, and at higher levels. Observe."

Guillermo's entire being pulsed with a wave of something that felt like his skin was being flayed from his body. His mechanical arm began to seize in overload and his legs convulsed wildly. He could barely utter a sound, his mouth contorted in a grimace of utter agony as his tongue pressed tight against his palate. The room began to spin around him as his stomach heaved and he curled into a fetal ball, but he fought through it, straightening out and flexing his muscles in defiance, muttering only a quivering groan.

The soft chuckle again.

"Do you then wish to eat?" asked Duuzra. "Or should you suffer the same fate as the Terran female?"

Guillermo stared at the bounty hunter, his eyes glaring, taking in a sharp breath.

"What did you say?"

Duuzra fluttered to the floor again and angled his v-shaped visor at Guillermo.

"The Terran woman was most uncooperative, and since we do not need many females for breeding stock, I flushed her out an airlock."

Guillermo flew at the bars, his hands grabbing them tight until a flash of sparks shot across his metallic arm and arced up to his shoulder. The Fraaz bounty hunter only turned and exited from the room leaving Guillermo to drive himself toward a self-induced blackout.

CHAPTER 34

Guillermo awoke to the acrid smell of anesthetic and discovered a tube running along his arm, stapled to his skin in three places. As he traced it with his eyes across his shoulder he knew from the itch that was developing that it was embedded in his neck. He tried to pull it free and found that it was attached via a snug metallic collar.

The Queen, according to his captor at least, was retaking Ontocca. Guillermo had tried to reason with the bounty hunter, to explain that his own planet Fraaz would be in jeopardy if she was allowed to grow her empire. Duuzra was unmoved, his answer bogged down in hatred for Terrans who had laid waste to his planet during the rebellion over a century ago.

"Who would want a wasteland?" Duuzra had growled before flitting out the door again to leave Guillermo hopelessly alone. Somehow he sensed a mark of sadness in the heavily modulated voice.

Guillermo hovered in the center of the hexagonal ball, the dirty metal walls of his cell visible in the dim light that shone down from above him. He thought about yelling again, but ended up muttering a few unintelligible words. He mused that his participation or lack of participation in the war was a failure regardless, his greater loss Mitsuki, but the utter hopelessness of his fate had begun to crush him beneath its gargantuan bulk.

After a few hours of maundering to himself, he decided he would make the last few hours of humanity memorable, and began to study the intricate workings of his cell.

His goal was suicide.

He had never seen this level of tech, not even on Ontocca. It didn't look like old Phaedran Empire tech that had been modified to suit another purpose like all the other tech in the Five Rims.

It was much more advanced.

Gravity inducers had been used for hundreds of years, but

this was a new kind of gravity control. As his eyes focused in on the bars of the polyhedral sphere he noticed that there were tiny gaps at the ends of each little bar, each held fast together by an unseen force field. Usually there was a generator nearby, something bulky that powered the field, but he could not see anything that even closely resembled one of these devices. As far as he could tell, the sphere was being held together with an unknown power source not connected via energy beams or power conduits.

Like a half-remembered dream, however, he felt a wave of grief as Mitsuki's face floated into his memory and his eyes again began to water, blurring his vision. He sickened at the nonchalant way that the bounty hunter had mentioned her death, his voice cold and unfeeling, as if discussing the death of a rodent in a household trap.

Rage then overshadowed despair and he had to at least kill this Fraaz v'oshtu for killing Mitsuki.

"Crulling bounty hunter has to be lying," he burbled. "I guess I'll kill myself after I find out if that shuhraad was telling the truth."

He began to explore his mechanical wrist. The inner workings had been exposed due to the rubberized housing burning away. He traced the small servos and flex-metal plating, and then noticed a small sliver of plasteel that had lodged itself in a knuckle joint.

He pulled at it, felt a staticky shock of pain that flickered there for a moment, then he clenched his teeth and pulled it free. He held it close to his eye, examining the small fragment momentarily before tapping it on an incisor. Holding it up to the dim light, he realized that it was a fragment of a control switch possibly, a few centimeters in length, but very thin and durable.

Tracing the tubing that floated from his neck out one of the spaces in the hexagonal bars, he could see that it was connected to a port on the wall outside his cage. The tube, constructed of a dense fiber weave, not easily severed by conventional use, could perhaps fail if he sliced at it with his little piece of plasteel.

He felt around his person, his fingers dancing across the pain-frequency belt that fit snugly around his waist. Looking left and right he could find no visible latch or buckle, but as his hand groped around behind him he could perceive a latch on the back just above his tail bone. Holding the plasteel shard carefully between the thumb and forefinger of his mechanical hand he stretched around, poking the back of the belt at the base of his spine until he felt the shard penetrate a slot. With the strength afforded him by the durasteel servos, he pressed in until he heard a crunch. He jiggled it left and right until something clicked and the belt fell away from him in the zero-g sphere.

He uttered a high pitched shout.

Quickly he grabbed the belt, examining it for any means of shorting out the bars, and to his dismay could not understand the technology used to build it. It had no visible seams or rivets, seemingly made from one solid piece of metal, yet it was flexible enough to wrap around his waist. It felt strangely light for such a bulky thing, its flexible housing a marvel of engineering. On a lark, he gripped the belt tightly on one end with his metallic hand and squeezed tight before swinging it at the bars just above his head.

He heard a vibrating roar, and the bars, each only as long as his hand, sparked and squealed. They released fiery energy that surely would have burned Guillermo's flesh had he touched them with his bare hands. As soon as the belt swung back to Guillermo the bars shimmered and returned to normal.

"Cherts yeah," he chortled.

Guillermo examined the belt for any damage while remaining completely still and listening for any thunderous reprisals or the skittering claws of the bounty hunter coming to check on his prey.

Nothing, only the caustic smell of ozone and the low rumble of space travel.

He assumed that the belt had not conducted the electric shock to his hand, which was a good thing, but he was still stuck in this cage. He decided he would experiment further, so he began twisting the belt in his hand, listening to the metal bend as his metallic fingers scraped and pulled at it. In desperation he squeezed the belt with his metallic hand and listened to the servos whine and the durasteel pop and strain under the stress of it.

SPROING!

A small crack had formed along the bottom seam of the belt and as he quickly pried the crack wider with his metal shard he could see a glowing crystal within the housing that gave off a strange odor, something like vinegar with a light tinge of ammonia. He reached a metal finger inside to pry it out and was thankful at once for being cursed with his prosthetic. A singular blue strand of energy leaped across the palm of his hand.

He pulled back, then dove in again, this time wrenching the crystal free from the belt. He had precious little understanding of how it worked, but he was sure this had something to do with the power supply…or it could be the thing that had dialed into his pain center. He had to know.

He held the square crystal in his hand, a thin blue shard, two centimeters square, and he noticed that the crystal had not been connected by any visible cables or power conduits. The crystal crackled, however, with an iridescent light that rippled and danced within its near-translucent interior. He had heard that crystalline power sources were sometimes adept at disrupting graviton emitters. He hoped that this would be his key to breaking this prison. He also hoped that the belt had been what had isolated the crystal from the bars.

Only one way to find out.

Escape or die trying.

With a few maneuvers learned in zero-g training, he managed to float toward the bars, the crystal held firmly in his metallic hand. He reasoned that if he were to trigger some sort of explosion then he would at least be able to repair his prosthetic arm easier than actual flesh.

There was plenty of metal around for the nanites.

As he floated closer to the bars, the very air around him

became charged with a static electric field that caused his mop of shaggy black hair to become a fright wig.

He thrust the fragment forward in his metal fist.

In seconds, millions of fragments of duraplast exploded from the sphere in the vicinity of his metallic hand, some of them causing him to close his eyes as they peppered his skin, some of them lodging themselves there. He cried out in pain, shielding his eyes with his forearm only to feel them dig into his flesh like ancient buckshot.

And then he was falling.

He hit the floor below with a thud. He lay motionless for a moment, the only sound the cascading shower of sparks and fragments that fell from the sphere to the floor as his convoluted plan managed to succeed.

Now to find my way out.

He stood up, then staggered forward, a twinge in his back screaming at him from the fall. He approached the door to the room only to see the dark angular shape of Duuzra emerge and growl at him from behind that black and red visor. The "ears" rotated back as the bounty hunter tackled Guillermo to the floor and knocked the wind from his chest.

Guillermo balled up his metallic fist and began to sledgehammer the Fraaz's helmeted head with blinding speed, the servos taking over and straining the framework that attached the arm to his torso. This compounded the pain in his back, but he continued, the hard metal of Duuzra's helmet sparking and deforming slightly. The bounty hunter reacted by using his superior weight to pin Guillermo to the floor.

"Your kind is truly annoying in its ability to sabotage the most complex devices," said Duuzra, his modulated voice calm yet breathy. "Now we will insure that you do not escape again. I shall lobotomize you a little early."

One of the small guns on Duuzra's armored shoulder rotated around and pointed at Guillermo's head. There was a loud blast as something exploded within the ship very close, perhaps a deck below them, and Guillermo saw for the first time what looked like the body language of surprise reflected on the bounty hunter.

"What's the matter, Fraaz," Guillermo spat. "Somebody else escape?"

Duuzra leapt from Guillermo and fluttered out of the room like a massive metal moth, the door slamming shut behind him. Guillermo shot to his feet and raced to the entrance, looking for some kind of switch that would open it, but found only a smooth wall on either side. Possibly the bounty hunter activated doors in his ship with his proximity or with a verbal cue.

Guillermo did not have time to think about it, because the ship lurched forward, throwing him to the floor again. The decking began to vibrate loudly, the outer hull squealing in protest with the unmistakable sound of uncontrolled re-entry. Something else exploded several decks above this time, and the engines that had been squealing suddenly stopped. As he scrambled across the floor he heard the horrifying silence of free-fall, then the bone-crushing crunch of a crash-landing.

Then all went black.

CHAPTER 35

"Wake up!"

Someone was shaking him, and as he blinked a swollen eye, he discerned the shape of someone in the darkness, his nose filled with the strange odor of molten metal. He felt hands fumbling at his clothes and then grabbing at his collar, and he heard a grunt as the person began to pull him along. He stumbled to his feet, waving his rescuer off with his hand and then using his blackened fingers to try to prevent the thick smoke from causing his eyes to water even more.

He staggered forward in the darkness, trying not to breathe in the bitter smoke, and as he cut to the left around a corner he saw a gaping hole in the hull and brilliant sunshine beyond. His rescuer was ahead of him, feeling along the walls as if blind, and as he doddered out onto a barren landscape of grey dirt and half-buried twisted structures he rubbed his eyes and stared blankly at Mitsuki.

"Serves you right," she said, pointing at his arm.

He looked down and saw that his metallic arm was sheared off at the elbow leaving a twisted tangle of nano-cabling and micro-servos. He only shrugged and then looked back at Mitsuki, his eyes narrowing.

"I'm alive," he said. "You? That bounty hunter said he threw you out an airlock."

That irresistible smirk crossed her lips.

"He tried."

Guillermo crouched as something within the ship coughed out a low thump, and he backed away from the wreckage and stared up at the teetering broken wings.

"You think he made it?"

"No…I don't know," she said. "It's possible. I was in one of the vents and he shot past me toward the back of the ship right before everything went to chert."

He stared at her, partly marveling at her sudden use of Guajiin profanity.

"How?"

"I just shimmied out to the engine room and started pulling things apart," she said, placing a bleeding finger in her mouth. "Uh ship did duh resht."

"Ok. He said he flushed you out an airlock is all."

"Yeah, that," she said, squeezing the bleeding finger and licking it once. "Can we get going? If we are going to be an arranged couple, then I suppose we'd better get on our merry way."

Guillermo only laughed, staring at his shredded arm again.

She's alive.

"We need to get away from here. If he's still kicking he'll want to recapture his prey, and he was using tech I've never seen before."

They crawled up a steep embankment of sand, their feet bogging down with the effort, and she had to pull him along as he could only use one arm to help with locomotion. As they reached the edge of the crater formed by the ship, they turned to look at a long scar that cut through the desert, the mangled ship a heap of blackened, smoking wreckage near them.

Lying in the middle of the twisted metal of Duuzra's ship were the vacant eye sockets and nasal cavity of the ornamental skull carved on the bow.

Guillermo's eyes rose to see something flailing beyond the wreckage.

"It's him," he said, starting off along the rim of the crater. "I'm going to finish the job."

"Or he'll finish you," Mitsuki growled, grabbing what was left of his arm. "Don't do two foolish things in one day. You don't have a weapon anyway."

He pulled away from her and bared his teeth.

"I don't need any!"

Just then a high-pitched squeal echoed across the wasteland. Guillermo fell to the powdery grey dust, his one hand covering an ear, his mouth agape. It was the screech of several hundred beings, and soon the brightness of the day was clouded by a fluttering mass of Fraaz who were descending on the wreckage like vultures on a carcass. Guillermo grit his teeth at the pain, and shielding his eyes from the sun with one hand, watched the creatures falling to the wreckage. Fraaz scavengers crawled over the jagged metal and began using tools to tear away loose parts and scrap. Before the Terrans could run, two Fraaz plopped down next to them and screeched out a warning, each wearing shoulder mounted autonomous projectile rifles that were loaded with multi-barbed harpoons.

"Terrans!" one of them shrieked, his dagger-like teeth flashing. "More for the brood!"

One of the quarter-meter long harpoons shot from the gun with a burst of compressed air and lodged itself in Guillermo's mechanical bicep. A thin filament line stretched tight.

Guillermo helplessly pulled at the line and was

lifted from the ground by the screeching Fraaz.
Guillermo soon dangled in the air, spinning around
aimlessly to watch Mitsuki slash the neck of one Fraaz
attacker with a nearby shard of metal before two of
them fell on her, cloaking her with their leathery wings.

He focused on where the Fraaz was carrying
him. In the distance rose a needle-like spire of rock
jutting out of the wasteland. Circling it, like a black
cloud-ring were the fluttering shapes of thousands of
Fraaz scavengers who guarded the entrance to their
cave city. He looked below him, and in the dust saw
pieces of combustion engine aircraft, advanced
architecture and the legendary hanging gardens. A flat
ruin of ash and rubble slowly passed by.

As the star that burned brightly in the Fraaz sky
began to fall beneath the wrecked horizon, Guillermo
and Mitsuki were carried deep within the spire. Once
inside, the Fraaz who carried them folded their wings
in a free-fall. Guillermo felt his organs convulse as they
dropped deep under the surface of the planet through a
cavernous hole to a cool world underneath. It was a
world of fires lit by the sewage gasses, twisted patchwork vehicles cobbled together, and domiciles that
hung from cave ceilings made from the detritus of a

nuclear wasteland.

Soon the two of them found themselves within rusty barred cages with nothing but a shredded fungus for bedding, surrounded by hundreds of Terrans who stared at the newcomers with blank eyes and gaping mouths.

CHAPTER 36

Guillermo and Mitsuki sat on the floor of their cage surrounded by a herd of gibbering Terrans, some of them drooling, but the vacant stares and gaping mouths told them a story that was quickly becoming the fate of their race. Each Terran wore a simple tunic, smeared with filth, ragged along the edges. A heavy-duty collar encircled their necks, each one with a red light that blinked on and off in a strangely festive way, a festival celebrated in hell. None were manacled, and Guillermo and Mitsuki were allowed to sit unrestrained inside the cage. Darkness surrounded the outside of their prison with only faint dots of light in the distance and the periodic shrieks and flapping of wings to indicate that they were not alone.

"What do you think they have planned?" asked Mitsuki, her voice nearly a whisper as she examined a scabbed-over gash on her forearm.

When she spoke the nearby Terrans scurried away, the sound of Terran speech seeming to frighten them.

"No idea," Guillermo replied as he played with one of the broken micro-servos on his mangled arm.

The harpoon had been hastily removed, leaving his arm in worse shape than before.

"Whatever they want, I guess. I wish we'd stop being the ones who pay for our ancestor's mistakes. Just want to get the crull out of here...maybe find that place beyond the ion cloud that Zuraal was talking about...find a place to settle down."

"Last man on Terra," said Mitsuki with a slight breath of a laugh. "Never forget."

Suddenly they were bathed in a new and blinding blue light that caused them to shield their eyes. The lobotomized Terrans in the cage gibbered louder, mostly moans and screams. First Mitsuki then Guillermo stood to their feet to embrace whatever new terror was descending on them. Quite literally it did descend in the form of three Fraaz who fluttered to the floor of the cage armed with their back-mounted harpoon guns. Guillermo noticed that the harpoons were actually controlled by a series of thin cables that ran through some conduits on a harness they wore. Subtle movements would aim and fire them.

"Grab them," said an albino Fraaz in the center, his muzzle covered with tumors, his left eye a vacant socket. "Process them."

Mitsuki immediately dropped low into a fighting stance, but Guillermo reached for her with his gnarled arm.

"Just go along with it," he said, keeping eye contact with the albino. "We'll see where this goes."

The two of them were carried up and out of the cage, held by the feet of the two other Fraaz. As they hung upside down they could see the post-apocalyptic nature of this underground city through the gloom. The cave floor was littered with debris and storage containers, as Fraaz would simply drop items that they considered waste, but above them was where the real activity bustled. Thousands of makeshift structures hung from the ceiling, either carved into gigantic stalactites or anchored through them with heavy metal rods. Each building was a patchwork of rusted metals scavenged from the surface or from other places, and here and there grew a bioluminescent fungus that provided dim green light for a race that used their vision much less than their hearing and sense of smell.

"You ok?" Guillermo shouted to her.

"Never better," she replied, her arms dangling. "You?"

"I've had worse."

This caused Mitsuki to utter a mad fit of laughter, but Guillermo knew that it was laughter born from desperation, from not knowing whether or not their brains were about to be scooped out or if they were going to be fed to one of the many predatory creatures that lived deep within these caves.

Guillermo had heard vague stories.

Much of the world of the Fraaz came as a surprise to Guillermo, anyway, because he had thought that the Fraaz were wiped out in the war, that their world had been so badly damaged with fusion, neutron and archaic nuclear weapons that nothing could survive there. That, as he could see, was only partially true.

They circled a small underground lake for a few moments, a coal-black body of still water. Foraging along the shore lumbered a herd of one of the few herbivores on Fraaz, the elephantine Auktaar. A four legged beast, its triangular torso was topped with an onion-shaped head sprouting a mass of tentacles that it used to forage the various poisonous plants growing along the bank. When Guillermo and Mitsuki were dropped unceremoniously to the cave floor the Auktaar stampeded away, its cries a muffled gurgle that echoed from the cave walls.

The Terrans were immediately surrounded by several Fraaz soldiers who plopped to the ground from above. A larger Fraaz reclining on a floating bed of silken pillows emerged from the darkness, his lips at one point burned away and his left wing atrophied and covered in tumors.

"You are the first Terrans to arrive on Fraaz on your own in centuries," the crippled Fraaz hissed. "I am curious as to how you made it here...or what your plans might be to infiltrate my clutch."

Guillermo tried to stand but was forced to his knees by the sudden and painful strike from a nearby guard.

"No plans," Guillermo said calmly, yet his voice could not mask the tremor. "Just wanted to see if the stories were true about your lovely vacation planet."

At this, he heard the deafening staccato screeching that passed for Fraaz laughter.

"Bring the collars," said the reclining Fraaz. "You will be slaves to Uaheet."

As the Fraaz handlers skittered forward to subdue the two Terrans, Guillermo raised his hands.

"You always speak of yourself in the third person?" Guillermo asked. "That's not a very good trait, you know. Kind of shows —"

And then they were set upon, held down. They did their best to struggle as scratchy collars were applied. When the collars clicked into place he heard the faint hum and whir of something deadly within and the little red light began to blink on and off in a slow rhythm. It lluminated the ground before them in a soft but ominous hue.

"This will make you more agreeable," said Uaheet as if reading from a script, a script he had read a thousand times. "However, if you struggle and are rendered unconscious by the collar, as you Terrans are so fond of doing, we will proceed to the surgery. Then you will be absolutely compliant, if not harder to train."

"Can I get one that matches my shirt?" asked Mitsuki, and Guillermo turned to her, a grin cracking his dirt-smudged face.

"Take the female to my warren," Uaheet droned as he twitched one atrophied finger along his shriveled wing. "The male can toil in the lower levels if he is not eaten by a kluudraa. Prepare my craft."

As several lights along Uaheet's skiff suddenly came to life Guillermo noticed that two Terran males were pushing him along, their skinny bodies a result of malnourishment, but they were strong enough to nudge the fat Fraaz along. Mitsuki was being prodded by two Fraaz guards as she followed the warlord to his "warren". Guillermo stood and then reached for his collar only to feel it set every nerve in his body on fire. He let go, but before he could utter another word he felt his ankles being grabbed as he was hoisted aloft into the darkness.

After a brief visit to the warlord's throne room where he was treated to a speech by Uaheet where his race was belittled and mocked, they flew him deep within the cave where his new job awaited him.

It turned out that working in the lower levels meant sewer duty.

CHAPTER 37

Guillermo stood at the bottom of a chasm, the only light a green hue produced by bioluminescent fungus that grew along the slimy walls. A steady flow of liquid rushed around him, but he knew from the smell that it was not water. He stood knee deep in it, and his given job was to clear a nearby outlet that would clog with waste periodically. All he could think about was how to get out before his legs and feet succumbed to the horrid bacteria present in the sewage.

He began clearing the outflow spout with his bare hand, and suddenly pulled back in pain when it scraped across a shard of metal that hung from the opening, long since rusted and useless. His eyelashes batted at the steady blink of red from his collar which periodically illuminated the darkness in front of him, and he noticed something moving to his left. He thought he was alone, but one never knew what lurked in the sewers of a Fraaz underground city. It surged closer, and he sloshed backward in the soup as a pockmarked and rotted corpse of a Terran slave bobbed toward him. It bounced off of his leg, the skin cold and covered in a viscous brown paste.

He fought another series of dry heaves and the stink from the sewer was beginning to make him feel light-headed. He looked up into the aperture above to see his three Fraaz guards hanging like bags of skin, their wings folded around them as they observed his torture. He shouted various epithets at them, but either they did not speak Terran or they did not care, and he reasoned that the latter was probably true.

A spark flared on his collar and the little red light burned brightly for a few extra moments before winking out.

He stopped for a moment, fearing to touch the collar again, and then simply rolled his eyes downward to see if he could notice what had caused it to spark so.

The light winked on.

Otherwise he saw nothing.

He continued, clearing the filth from the drain until a putrid flow of grainy sewage billowed forth and splashed across his face. He puffed and spit, and then the collar sparked again, this time the light going out completely, now the only illumination the eerie glow from the fungus. He reached up to touch the collar, reached too far in the dark and touched its smooth surface, but was stunned to find that it did not bite him like before.

Something was happening.

The nanites.

It was the only thing that could be doing this. He held his mangled arm out, trying to see it in the dim light, and noticed that it was longer, that the wrist was forming and that the micro-servos were beginning to knit back together. The little buggers were using the metal of the collar to reform his arm.

This news caused him to work a little faster, and he wondered when the guards would notice that his collar's activation light wasn't blinking anymore and swoop down to deal with it. He continued to work, keeping one eye on the Fraaz guards who hung above him in the darkness and the other on the repair progress of his arm. He knew that if the nanites had deactivated the collar that he could leave any time, but he had to devise a way past the guards, past the horde of Fraaz who would come hunting him if he tried to escape.

And then he saw his answer.

It would be bad.

He reached for the drain spout with his trembling hand and found the shard, pulling at it until it squeaked and then gave way, but it sliced him for the trouble. He shouted up into the crevasse above.

"I need water! Water!"

He saw something stirring above in the darkness, but then he closed his eyes, took a deep breath of ammonia soaked air and submerged himself in the filthy sewage, his nose burning and his mind reeling with the very idea of what he was doing.

He felt a stirring as something hit the surface of the sewage above him. It began to feel around in the muck for him. He lashed out with the shard, stabbing the Fraaz in the lower abdomen, driving it deeper as he shoved forward and used his feet to steady himself on the slippery floor beneath the sewage. He heard a screech and then he wrapped his arm around the shoulder. He held to the Fraaz, his bleeding fingers scrambling for purchase, as the Fraaz began to flap his thick wings and rise higher and higher. His captor was screeching to his fellow guards, and even though Guillermo could not speak his language he knew that the next few moments would be key.

He wrapped his legs around his jailer's waist and squeezed tight with his thighs for dear life, then twisted to the side, causing his victim to scream something nearly inaudible. The Fraaz climbed higher, spinning faster. The other two guards reacted, their frantic cries echoing off of the walls as they circled the pair, their harpoon guns aiming but not firing. Apparently Guillermo's victim was their leader.

"You and me are going to hell together," Guillermo barked, the madness exploding out of him, ignoring the goo sliding down his face and across his lips. "And it'll be a vacation home compared to this dump!"

The Fraaz did not respond, but now his lieutenants were swooping closer, and just as Guillermo began to feel the heavy breeze of their passing, his victim slammed into the wall and then dropped to a nearby platform, rolling across the metal floor to try and dislodge the Terran from his body. The guard slapped Guillermo with one wing, and then bent his body around to gnash at him with his long, sharp teeth. Guillermo ducked, then crawled on top of his victim's back and began punching it again and again, pounding madly, franticly at the base of his jailer's skull. Soon he could see that the space between the Fraaz's cold eyes was wrinkling, the tip of one wing twitching, but now the other two captors landed on the platform nearby and were rushing toward him teeth bared and slender fingers on their wings grasping at him.

His mangled left arm now formed a pointy mess at the severed wrist made of micro-servos and monofilament cables. He used it to stab at the first Fraaz to get close enough. The creature hesitated, nostrils flaring, then bit down on his forearm and gnawed on it, a mixture of drool and blood spraying Guillermo's face as one of the long teeth broke off in the fray. The other was crawling the wall at the edge of the platform, the harpoon gun focusing in on his position, and he reasoned that this final attacker would be less concerned about collateral damage.

He had to move fast.

The Fraaz gnawing on his arm was standing erect, a position not natural for his kind, and Guillermo placed his hand on the furry throat and pushed, his boots sliding on the platform as both of them toppled over. His attempt to pin his attacker was short lived, however, as he heard a sharp concussive blast of air and felt a chip of duracrete strike his cheek, his head only inches away from an embedded harpoon. A shadow strangled out the dim green light that barely illuminated the platform and he was suddenly covered by the leathery wings of the other Fraaz.

"I guess you both want to go to hell with me then!" he roared, and with one motion ripped his arm free from the Fraaz's mouth and began stabbing the creature under him again and again with its jagged wrist, the creature's cries nearly deafening as it flopped around on the platform.

He could feel the other one still on top of him, so he slid to the side and tried to roll over, but to no avail. The final attacker was determined to kill him, its long fingers along the wings grasping and slashing at him.

And then there were the teeth.

He struck out with his only weapon, his sharpened wrist tearing a hole in the Fraaz's right wing. It screeched in pain, retaliating by biting his fleshy shoulder and tearing a jagged wound there. Blood sprayed the side of Guillermo's face as it screamed. Straining with everything he had he managed to fold into a fetal position, then kicked out with his feet to throw it off of him momentarily. Before he could get to his feet, however, the creature was scurrying toward him, its teeth gnashing. It shouldered him to the ground again, then breathed a heavy groan and slumped to the platform.

The Fraaz lay still, and underneath the beast lay Guillermo, his jagged wrist buried deep within the creatures's abdomen.

Guillermo crawled out from under the Fraaz, his metallic arm scraping on the duracrete, his shoulder bleeding heavily, and he stood on wobbly legs to gape over the edge of the platform at the river of sewage faintly visible in the glow of the underground fungi. With a heavy sigh he looked above him at the fissure, a soft light far at the top, and then he wondered how he was going to climb out with a severed arm and a fresh, bloody shoulder wound.

And then he saw his answer.

CHAPTER 38

Mitsuki knelt on the floor, her arms aching as she scrubbed back and forth with a foul, dirty sponge. Uaheet, this clutch's warlord, a bloated, tumor-covered mess of a Fraaz, lay on his hover skiff a few meters away from her. His twisted mouth chattered in the throes of deep slumber.

She had attempted removing her collar once, and only once. That was enough. The shock she received from it was something connected to her nervous system rather than a normal electric shock, and she could feel it throughout her body.

Shuffling around the throne room were five filthy Terrans that Uaheet apparently kept as pets. She reasoned that it was only a matter of time before she would join them in their lobotomized oblivion. She wondered what was happening to Guillermo, whether he was still alive. That line of thought usually caused her to remember the fact that she might be free if she'd remained in the jungle on Ontocca.

"Scrub harder," hissed a Fraaz handler, his voice low so as not to wake the warlord. "Uaheet will eat your limbs if you do not make the floor spotless."

She only turned and nodded, trying to prevent
the crippling pain that would come from the collar if
she didn't obey immediately. She did as she was told.

The cavernous room would take some time to
clean. The floor stretched out to form several ledges
where large open windows looked out onto the cave
below. The throne room was sparsely furnished, as
Fraaz did not have much need for it, but protruding
from the ceiling were several hooks and rings where the
warlord's lieutenants would often hang and slumber.
She assumed that the only reason Uaheet did not hang
from the ceiling was because his injuries from long ago
prevented him from flying or from climbing to the
perches.

Her handler, a gluttonous blob of fur with wings,
his teeth dripping drool, only stared at her from his
rusty ring on the ceiling and barked orders at her in a
low growl so as not to wake the warlord. Actually,
Mitsuki couldn't understand how the warlord did not
wake himself with his own snoring.

She scrubbed the duracrete floor, dipping now
and again from a brackish bucket of water, lifting and
setting it down so it didn't make a scraping noise. She
moved toward the window, and as she came closer she

gasped at the height of Uaheet's throne room, far above any other dwelling, nestled in the very apex of the cavern. She could make out lights along the roof of the cavern where several other dwellings hung like upside-down mushrooms growing from the roof of the cave. Faintly visible in the green illumination of the cave fungi, each of them were patchworks made of rusted metal scraps of durasteel welded together in various geometric shapes and patterns.

The Fraaz had made something remarkably beautiful from the wreckage that her people had centuries ago wrought on them. Perhaps it was fitting that her race were now the subservient and mindless brutes who shuffled around, performing menial tasks of cleaning the lavatory and the large concave dish that the warlord called a bathtub.

And then she felt pain.

She dropped the sponge and nearly kicked over the bucket as her body was wracked by a fire coursing through her veins.

"Do not daydream by the window, Terran," came the thunderous growl of Uaheet as he released a button on his brooch using a gnarled digit on a broken wing. "We will not have my new slave falling from the palace window…or were you thinking of ending it?"

The pain subsided, and only then could she respond.

"No, my lord," she said, the briefing she had received about etiquette still fresh in her mind. "I was only admiring your kingdom."

Uaheet rolled over to face her, his pillows shifting beneath his bulk.

"Kings wear crowns, born to rule that which is not earned," the warlord replied. "I have killed all who oppose me."

The handler, dropping to the floor with a breezy thud, skittered to the base of the throne and stretched completely prone on the floor, his wings spread flat.

"My lord," he said, his voice a soft purr. "Allow me to take my leave of you. I desire to take this new slave to the training area to fully process her…train her for your service."

The warlord, his pale skin flaking as he moved, turned his triangular head slowly to face Mitsuki.

"No," he said. "Leave her with me. I would like to further converse with her. Terrans have a complex mind, and it is pleasing to explore their capacity before we do the surgery."

Mitsuki could not read Fraaz expressions but she could sense the handler's displeasure.

"As you wish, my lord," said the handler, and he rose to shuffle past Mitsuki, his wing slapping her painfully as he exited the window. Soon she could hear the leathery pop of those wings as he sailed away in the darkness.

After a moment of silence, a moment that Mitsuki felt was more uncomfortable than being in the middle of a whiptail den, the warlord turned to her, his gnarled face displaying a dead-rat grin.

"Come closer," he said plainly, without intonation. "I want to get a better look at you."

Cautiously she stood, her legs wobbling a bit at first, and then she moved closer to him, her hand still gripping the sponge as if it were a child's security blanket. As she approached, she held the sponge in both hands tight to her chest, the odorous water soaking her tunic, yet she did not feel the coolness of the water, only the blazing fear of what might happen to her if she did not comply.

Yesterday she had discovered how capable the guards in the hallway were at subduing her quickly, but it was Uaheet who possessed the dreaded button control to her collar.

She quivered at the base of his "throne" which was nothing more than a mound of pillows piled on an old rusty hover skiff, one repulser node flickering in the gloom. He shifted forward, his tumor-covered and atrophied wing trying its best to help move his bulk. Soon he was inches from her, face to face, and she could smell the foul breath wafting across his jagged yellow teeth.

"I have eaten your kind before, Terran," he grunted. "Quite tasty you are, but especially the little ones, your young. They are tender and not so stringy."

She squirmed, her eyes squeezing shut as he extended a long tongue, its wet saliva dripping. It slid along her neck and then her cheek, then she felt it curve around to the back of her shoulder. She tried not to shudder, but found the involuntary reflex too much to withstand. This seemed to please the warlord, and he retracted his tongue, sinking back onto his pillows, his little atrophied wing fluttering with what could only be excitement.

"Excellent," he chortled. "I will have much fun fattening you up for a feast. Now get back to scrubbing the floor...I do not want to feel grit on my skin when I have to walk. I cannot fly because my grandparents had to exist in that ruination your kind wrought upon my planet."

She took three steps back, turned and moved quickly to the bucket where she soaked the sponge and continued her work. She remembered the whiptails, when she crept into their den to rescue Guillermo, and reasoned that she was in better company now.

At least the Fraaz could reason.

She took the risk.

"Your society seems to have risen from the ashes, so to speak," she managed, then flinching when he moved suddenly.

He let out a low, vibrating, high pitched sound that could only be a laugh.

"Of course," he said. "Our kind have managed to find a light in the nuclear darkness, and it is only by our will to survive that we have built this city. There are many like it across the wasteland, but this one is bigger and better than the rest. Soon we will have the means to leave this planet again and find the rest of your kind. Perhaps we will eat them as well."

Cautiously she rose, then moved to the window where she knelt and scrubbed the floor, staring again at the vast cavern below and realizing that she could never survive a jump from this height.

Perhaps she didn't care to survive.

She considered it again.

"There are not any more of us," she said, her breath becoming rapid from the work. "My companion…Guillermo…was the last Terran of the bug home world, and the Ontoccans kept a few of us, but they are gone. I am afraid that Guillermo and I are the last Terrans left…at least those who still have our minds intact."

At this, the warlord slid onto the floor and scurried over to her with remarkable speed. Before she could react he had pinned her to the floor with his one functioning wing. The other Terrans scattered, most of them forcing open the rusting door and then running out past the guards, gibbering and drooling.

The two Fraaz guards peered around the doorframe, their eyes black, and then one of them fluttered off to retrieve the slaves.

Uaheet pressed Mitsuki to the hard floor, the duracrete cool and slippery from the soapy water.

"That is a lie, Terran!" Uaheet shouted, his gnashing teeth inches from her face. "There is talk among my kind of the Terran's return! Of how they will emerge from the void and enslave us all again, the Five Rims races as well as the Terrans who are left in this place! My brother has shown me their traces! Their scouts have even been *here*!"

She attempted to shrink from the warlord's jaws, but his tongue came out again and tasted her skin.

"How do you know this?" she cried, her eyes squeezing shut so hard that she saw faint sparkles.

Without warning he let her go, his body shrinking back away from her. He seemed to calm himself, fighting the overwhelming urge to eat her right off the floor. One remaining Terran stood against the far wall, his eyes wide, his mouth agape, but he said nothing…could say nothing.

"My brother," Uaheet said coldly, his head low to the floor. "My brother Duuzra, who left our clutch long ago, hunts bounties for anyone who has enough chids. He told me of the Terrans from beyond…how he fought one of them while chasing a bounty…how he almost died when this warrior from beyond the ion cloud nearly ended his life."

Uaheet bellowed a wheezy laugh.

"But my brother outsmarted him…stole some of

his tech, he did…a ship."

She sat up, and in her haste nearly kicked over the bucket. She knew Duuzra, the bounty hunter who had brought them to this wasteland. She absently wondered if he was still alive and then hoped that he was not.

Prayed that he was not.

The things he did to her while she was in his med-bay, when he thought she was unconscious.

"My brother is a disgraced warrior," Uaheet continued, rising up to peer down his tumored nose at the Terran female. "And for his trouble he was forever crippled by his encounter with this Terran. Serves him right as he is…a shameful disgrace. He has turned his back on our ways."

The warlord's one good eye widened then as a sound outside the window grew louder and louder, a sharp whine of an engine. Mitsuki took to her feet and ran as something blasted through the open window of the throne room and skidded across the floor to crash into the throne, a ball of fire erupting from the base of it.

They all heard a Terran scream.

"Outrage!" screeched Uaheet as he flailed his

atrophied wing. "Guards!"

The two Fraaz guards scurried through the open door toward the ball of billowing black smoke, but up from the heap came Guillermo, shedding the booster jetpack that had transported him here. He fell to the floor to put out the flames that were burning the back of his shirt.

"Crull it all!" he screamed as a wash of soapy brown water hit him across the back. Mitsuki stood near him holding her bucket.

"Ghaaa!" growled Uaheet, his atrophied wing fluttering in protest. "Kill them both!"

The two guards began to flap their wings at the smoke, but it only caused the wreckage of the throne to smolder and the embers to produce more flames. Guillermo grabbed Mitsuki and they backed behind the throne, and she noticed that his left cheek was red and glistening from an awful burn.

"You have a plan, I guess?" she said over the screeching of the guards.

"Not really," he said. "My collar doesn't work anymore, so that's a plus."

The Terrans huddled behind the throne as the two guards began to circle it, their screeching used to bounce sound off of the walls in search of their prey. Through the smoke she saw a Terran lying on the floor near the far wall, his legs and arms sprawled out in a helpless pose.

"What have we done?" she shouted, tears beginning to stream due to the smoke and her rage. "We have to find the others!"

"One thing at a time," Guillermo said. "You think one of these brutes can carry both of us?"

Before she could speak, he was rushing the guard nearest the window, and with a strike of his newly formed metal fist he managed to uppercut the Fraaz. A wing tried to wrap around Guillermo and a harpoon bolt fired aimlessly at the ceiling. Guillermo was grappled for the Fraaz's legs and pushed him toward the window.

"Grab my waist, girl!" he shouted. "I bet he'll slow our descent!"

She didn't think, only obeyed. She ran for him, but then felt the unbearable pain of the collar and knew that Uaheet was pressing the trigger. She struggled, falling to the floor and writhing, her limbs seizing in a mad dance of fiery pain.

Guillermo stopped, turned to face her briefly,

doubled the Fraaz over with a well placed kick, and then ran to her. His fingers fumbled on the collar which only made her squirm all the more. The room was filling with toxic smoke from the jet pack booster. He peered through the gloom and could just see the bleached skin of Uaheet. Rushing through the burning throne, kicking ash and embers as he went, he used his metal fist to strike the warlord across the jaw.

Uaheet spat a crimson spray of blood across the floor.

"I will eat you raw!" he gurgled, and pushed Guillermo back to the embers which were now forming little dancing flames.

Guillermo tried to push back, but the Fraaz was too strong, and he began jack-hammering at the warlord's head with his fist. This only seemed to anger Uaheet who slapped at Guillermo with his good wing, the claw-like fingers on the elbow wrapping around Guillermo's head. The warlord gripped tightly, pulling down and scratching across the Terran's burned face, stopping just below his right eye. With a string of profanity, Guillermo punched through pale skin. His voice nearly shredding with a scream, he struggled and then pulled back a bloody mass of meat.

Uaheet dropped into the flames as Guillermo fell further backward, back toward a wailing Mitsuki, as the fire began to sizzle and pop the warlord's flesh.

With his remaining strength, his legs nearly buckling, Guillermo grabbed Mitsuki in his arms and rushed through the doors of the throne room, into a long hallway lined with frightened and mentally incapable Terrans.

CHAPTER 39

The Terrans in the hallway only stared at him,
their drooling mouths like black "O's".

Mitsuki's head lolled from side to side as he shot
down the hallway. Hot on their heels was a very
determined Fraaz guard who pushed past the
frightened Terrans, screeching out possible Fraaz
epithets. Guillermo had to find a way out, a way back
to the wasteland perhaps, or to a ship.

The Terrans scurried away from them, grunting
or babbling, but none of them helped, and some of them
he had to push out of the way as he struggled to
navigate the hallway which soon ended at a huge hole.
It gave him a great view of the outlying dwellings that
clung to the ceiling, but did not offer a ladder, an
elevator or even a crulling slide to get down to the
ground.

He looked behind him.

The Fraaz was still coming for him.

He set Mitsuki down.

His eyes flitted around the opening and he saw a
few cables along the edge attached to some kind of
bucket or ball nearby. He couldn't tell if it was

anything in the dim light, but he grabbed at it and it came loose, sprinkling him with something that stunk, but not as bad as he currently smelled. He pulled, and it detached from the wall, and then he crouched, wrapping it around and under Mitsuki's arms and waist, tying it tight, then around his own waist and over his shoulder.

Turning, he faced his enemy, arms outstretched as if receiving a ball in a sporting event.

But there was rookie fear in Guillermo's eyes.

The Fraaz charged him, and Guillermo reached out, grabbing handfuls of fur, twisting, and the three of them fell. The Fraaz screeched and flapped at the air. They were falling, falling. He could feel the cable tighten on his body, and he held on, hoping that the cable held. The constriction of the cable around his chest cut off his breathing, but he thanked the maker for it because it told him that Mitsuki was alive.

At least she was alive enough to fall to a horrible crushing death with him.

Attached to a screeching Fraaz.

The Fraaz's screeching was drawing other noises out of the dark as they fell. The cool wind rushed past them and he dared not look around him, focusing instead on holding fast to this beast's fur. He was going to ride this horror train to the end of the line, and he didn't care if he died. He didn't care about anything but Mitsuki and the mess he had gotten her into. In the madness of the fall, in that brief moment of spinning chaos, he promised that if they made it, he'd drop her off on a planet somewhere safe (if that was a real place) and let her live in peace.

Without him.

The Fraaz continued to flap his large leathery wings, and now Guillermo could see the ground, and it was littered with mounds of jagged metal. The city threw out whatever they did not need, and now the last Terran male in existence would be impaled on a Fraaz garbage heap.

"Flap your wings you crulling stooge!" Guillermo screamed.

The Fraaz tried to bite him, gnashing his teeth just inches from Guillermo's bleeding face.

"Yeah! Do your worst! Not good enough!"

The ground was approaching fast, and the Fraaz began to care more about self-preservation than trying to escape Guillermo's grasp. He grunted under the strain, his screeching silenced by the will to ascend.

The unforgiving ground with its piles of gnarled scrap metal inched closer and closer.

Remarkably, they were slowing.

Guillermo held on, the fist he was born with beginning to weaken, so he gripped tighter with the metal one. The Fraaz let out a growl that curdled Guillermo's blood. Now he had to figure out what to do if they survived, because this was one cranky guard he was clinging to.

"Thank you for flying chert-bag space lines," Guillermo said, his voice shaky. "Please make sure your seat backs and tray tables are in —"

And they were down, but the wind coughed right out of Guillermo's chest and he nearly blacked out as the huge guard fell on top of him and then began to flutter around. Guillermo shifted his weight, grunted loudly, and pulled himself from under a quivering wing, grabbing Mitsuki and dragging her behind.

The Fraaz had snagged a wing on a twisted piece of metal that protruded from his webbing like a dagger through a sheet of brown paper. The creature screamed, and though he flopped about his motions were sluggish with fatigue. Guillermo, without a word, scooped up Mitsuki and on legs that protested the pain scurried away from the injured Fraaz as the sound of screeching enemies began to gather above him.

In the gloom ahead he spotted a darker spot, a hole in the darkness that was much more black than the rest. As he approached it, he could see that it was indeed another cave entrance. He ducked into it and tried to remain as still as he could. Mitsuki did not have this problem, as she was completely motionless save for the slow rise and fall of her chest.

He waited for some time, and as long as he remained quiet and did not move it seemed that the Fraaz could not locate him in the dark. The creatures used echolocation to find their prey, but if the prey did not move and was very quiet, the prey might just survive to fight another day.

Or at least make it out of the clutch.

He whiled away the time working to remove the collar from Mitsuki's neck. It took some effort, and he nearly sent her into cardiac arrest once, but he managed to get it off.

The Fraaz search party didn't let up for hours, and eventually Mitsuki stirred, her eyes opening and then blinking heavily as she tried to see in the dim environ of the cave.

"Are we safe?" she whispered.

He didn't answer, but put his hand over her mouth, marveling secretly at the softness of her lips against his skin.

He pointed deeper into the cave, and they crouched low, moving silently in the darkness as they felt along. Soon they were in a place completely devoid of light. The darkness covered them like a cold damp blanket of wool. They continued on, however, their only option to go back into the Fraaz infested clutch. They had maimed and possibly killed the Fraaz warlord, so Guillermo figured they were crulled for sure.

Suddenly Mitsuki grunted, her shin banging into something metallic.

They felt around in the darkness, and Guillermo's eyes widened, feeling the unmistakable shape of a hover bike. It was one just like the model he had owned back on the bug home world. It felt cold against his skin, and damp, the dew from the cave condensing on its rusted metallic surface creating a grit that he could feel when he rubbed his fingers together. From memory, he began feeling for the activation switch, but couldn't seem to locate it, and then he felt the guns mounted on the front near the fuselage.

"It's a pre-rebellion bike," he whispered. "Look at this."

He waved his hand along the underside of the saddle and something glowed faintly in the darkness. It flickered, then died, then fired to life, and suddenly he could see the wall of the cave in front of him as several grisly somethings scurried away from the new pool of light.

Cautiously he climbed aboard and then Mitsuki behind him. He gingerly pushed the throttle forward a bit and found his way along the cave. It snaked toward an upward incline. Soon, a faint light began to appear ahead, and even though the engine of the ancient bike protested he pushed it on. As they neared the entrance something large and spindly pulled away from the wall and began to chase them. Mitsuki screamed and held on to him as he pushed the ratty engine of the bike along and dared not look back.

But she did, and her fear was heard in rapid gasps.

"It's so...so awful!" she shouted above the whine of the fusion engine.

"Ignore it!" he roared. "Just look at the light!"

They did.

They focused on it as it grew, but when they neared the edge, they saw that below the opening loomed a steep cliff, an incline much too steep to simply drive down without upending the bike.

Guillermo pushed the cranky throttle all the way.

CHAPTER 40

There is a moment in free fall when the body reacts to the sensation, increasing heart rate, skin temperature, and perspiration. The mind causes tunnel vision and the eyes dilate as if to say: "Why, in God's name would you do such a thing to me, you stupid v'oshtu?"

Guillermo held tight to the handlebars of the hover bike as it proceeded down on an 80 degree incline, and Mitsuki held fast to his waist as the two of them rumbled at an ever-increasing pace. He steered rapidly around hunks of wrecked metal ships and implements left over from the long-ago war. Selective hearing was another side-effect to free fall, and Mitsuki shouted in his ear a few words, only one of them understood, that caused him to divert his attention between the approaching obstacles and the sky above.

"Followed!"

Flooding from the crack in the mountain like a swarm of insects, a cloud of Fraaz warriors roared out of their warren to pursue the pair. Guillermo could not think about them as he madly considered how he was going to hide from them. For now he punched the throttle again even though it was redlining. As the terrain began to level off he could see in the distance an ancient Terran heavy cruiser, its bow jutting out of the desert sand like a gargantuan arrow head. He hung to a shred of hope that they could hide in its cavernous labyrinth of multiple decks. As the sand stung his face and threatened to blind him, stirred up by the stuttering engine of the hover bike, he heard the multiple zings of harpoons striking the ground around him.

They fell like rusty steel rain.

One of the Fraaz warriors swooped in beside him and executed a frighteningly graceful barrel roll, firing a harpoon diagonally at their engine. The velocity coupled with the energy field emitted by the fusion reactor prevented it from striking home. The next one would be more successful.

Guillermo hurt for a weapon, but his gaze was locked on the cruiser, and as he neared it he could see that it had been efficiently scavenged over time, its rusting hull a jagged landmark on an otherwise forgotten landscape. Something bumped the back of the bike, an overzealous Fraaz warrior, who fell to the ground, instantly destroying his wings in a tumbling mess far behind them.

A harpoon zinged close to Guillermo's head as he dodged left, then right. Desperately he shot for a hangar bay on the far side of the cruiser. The ancient landing ramp was as large as half a city block and pockmarked with jagged holes and mounds of sand. It lay open and neglected. There was a time long ago when it would have sent a chill of fear through any who saw it as the hordes of Terran shock troops would descend on a planet in order to dominate and enslave. He weaved around the holes and rocketed into the hangar, harpoons clanging on the landing ramp behind him as he found one of the many hallways that split off of the main dock.

Close behind him came the screeches of his enemy, their effort now focused on surrounding the ancient cruiser. He knew that they would try to flush him out. He had other plans.

"What are you doing?" Mitsuki exclaimed. "They will fall on this place like ch'udaa locusts on a hydroponics bay."

Guillermo slowed the bike, its engine beginning to fail. After a moment of puttering around the vacant hallways, the darkness swallowing them, he set his eyes on what he had been searching for.

"These ships were the biggest in the fleet back in the day," Guillermo offered, blinking his eyes in the gloom as they dismounted the bike. "Terrans are a cautious lot by nature. There has to be some kind of ship we could get running in here."

Mitsuki slid off the back of the bike then stood with her arms folded. Guillermo smiled at her out of reflex more than amusement. Her pouting lip was unconsciously driving him mad.

"This ship is picked over," she said, her voice low. "What makes you think there will be anything in here of use to us. We couldn't be more doomed."

He laughed, something she didn't hear from him often, and it caused her to offer a slight smile in spite of the situation.

"Yeah," he said, traipsing off to a nearby wall. "But I gotta try."

Her eyes widened, illuminated by a faint light that was blinking through the eons of rust and decay.

"What's that?" she asked, pointing to the wall.

He turned, placed his grease-stained hand against the metal, and it suddenly grew brighter, a soft blue orb.

"Activated by my DNA, I guess," he said. "Ok.

I'll bite."

He waved his hand around, then pressed down on the orb and something groaned within the decking as the wall split with a loud metallic crack and a vast room was revealed beyond. Very dim lights came to life within, the power cells barely alive after all this time, and they could make out a large vehicle beyond. It was a simple fuselage, the shape of a brick with a tapered end, and two triangular wings that jutted out from each side, but it was outfitted with several large guns, typical of old Terran war-tech.

They ran to it.

As they approached, they heard the cry of hundreds of Fraaz warriors who were growing closer. The Terrans did their best to ignore it as Guillermo used his DNA trick to activate the two-meter-wide landing ramp. It was a medium sized gunship, something probably not capable of FTL travel, but enough to get them off this rock or at least to safety.

They raced inside to the cockpit where two worn seats awaited them, and just as they closed the landing ramp several Fraaz warriors fluttered into the hidden hangar like moths looking for a flame. The ship was powering up, its power cells weak from decades of neglect, but Guillermo thought that it might have enough for escape velocity at least, and a little more still.

At least he hoped it would.

Mitsuki was touching a console in front of her, red and blue lights coming to life at her fingertips, and then she cleared her throat just as a Fraaz slapped the side of the plasteel canopy with a black wing.

"You think these weapons still work?" she asked.

She didn't have to wonder long. Her fingers danced across the rotted console and searing bolts of plasma shot out of a cannon mounted just under the cockpit, vaporizing several of their attackers. This caused the enemy to scramble, to thicken the swarm as more of them poured into the hangar. Guillermo slammed his metal fist on the console in front of him.

"Don't do that!" he shouted. "We need all the power we can muster to get out of here!"

He flipped the throttle, not much different from his old ship *The Terminarch*. After a couple of tense seconds where the engines nearly died, they lifted off the floor of the hangar.

Dusty fingers of light reached down from above as harpoons pinged harmlessly on the metal hull. Some of the Fraaz attempted to cling to the canopy, their angry faces a death-mask of hatred. The light came from an automatic door that had been triggered by unseen systems still stored somewhere. The hinges complained and nearly failed, but the ancient doors wobbled open just enough for them to hover out. The persistent Fraaz warriors clambered about their ship, some of them thudding into their plasteel canopy like giant bugs on a windshield.

He gave it the gas.

They rode the thermal updrafts for a while before cutting in the afterburners, or rather afterburner, and they managed to limp far above the atmosphere, dropping Fraaz warriors along the way. He cut the engines once they reached vacuum, pushing forward on maneuvering thrusters, most of them inoperable, and was comforted to realize that the life support still worked, even if the fans coughed out the musty smell of age.

Mitsuki sneezed.

"Now what?" she said, rubbing her button nose and staring out the cockpit dome at the yellowed surface of Fraaz far below. "I suppose we hitch a ride with someone now?"

"We have some time before the life support goes," he said evenly. "That's all we have. I don't know how we will live past today, but at least we are alive right now. That's all that matters."

"What matters is that I'm starving," she said. "And it's cold."

He jostled around. A metal fist shot back at her grasping a small packaged rectangle. She held out her hand, thought about it, then took it.

"A protein bar?" she said, then sniffed the golden wrapper and her tongue shot out in a gag reflex. "Where did you keep it? Next to your butt?"

"They had me working in a sewer," he said matter-of-factly. "The wrapper should have protected it."

He turned around in his seat and leveled his eyes at her.

"And you're going to complai—"

She was eating it.

He turned back around and stared out into the void of space, the myriad stars like little candles burning in a monastery, somehow peaceful considering his situation. He always found this sight calming, as if he was born to live out here, not on some bug planet or anywhere else.

He saw in the distance the strange undulating purple haze that was the visible spectrum of the ionic cloud. It was a dangerous expanse not far from Fraaz where the Terrans of the Phaedran Empire had been exiled, had been left to die.

He wondered.

He wondered about the Shibboleth, the place Zuraal told them about, the place where he and Mitsuki apparently had been born. Perhaps the old Guajiin had been lying to him, however, just another disappointing twist of fate. If they could find a working ship, get through the cloud somehow, they could possibly find kinship with this group of Terrans.

If they existed at all.

If they weren't monstrous and malevolent.

She shared the last fourth of the protein bar with him. They told old stories, made small talk, and drifted into a conversation that amounted to a half-hearted attempt at flirting. After an hour, or what seemed an hour without a chrono, they drifted off to sleep. Before he closed his eyes he took one more look at the strange purple hue of the ionic cloud. He thought through some ideas as to what to do next, how they might procure a better mode of travel, then gave up, instead giving in to the sandman.

They slept so soundly that they didn't hear the tractor beam lock on, at least until the docking clamps made the hull pop.

CHAPTER 41

"Are you cursed?" she shouted, a loud grinding sound nearly drowning out her voice.

"Yeh...I don't *think* so," he stammered, moving his hands over the console in front of him. "Maybe."

Through the cockpit canopy they could see they were inside some kind of zero-gravity hold, a large grey box, the planet below visible through two heavy doors hanging open in front of them. Massive docking clamps held their gunship tightly in an iron grasp.

"That noise," she said, inching out of her seat. "It's coming from back there, near the entrance ramp. I think they, whoever they are, are drilling through the bulkhead."

He set the engines to cycle and then stared back behind Mitsuki, looking into a room just beyond the cockpit.

"There was some loose deck plating back there," he said, pointing aft. "Get under it."

She didn't argue, but threw up her hands as they shuffled back to the room behind of the cockpit. He pulled up a rusted deck plate to find a small storage space big enough for the two of them.

"Where did you get this bright idea?" she asked, dropping down into the hole.

"Saw it in a holo-vid once," he offered, wiping the sweat from his eyes with a dirty hand. "It worked for them. Maybe we got a shot."

The grinding noise became louder, and just as they secured the decking above their heads and crouched in silence, there was a loud bang. Smoke and sparks shot into the room through tiny holes in the deck plate. Guillermo stared at Mitsuki for a moment, but all she could do was look up as the pattering of exoskeletal feet tromped onto their gunship and began pacing the floors.

He looked up again and clearly saw the armored shapes of bug soldiers as they swept through the ship, plasma guns raised, their mandibles clicking out a uniform pattern.

Then he saw Dervish.

She stood directly above him on the deck plating, her electro-glaive stowed away on her belt, and he knew that by the posture of her body she was reaching out with her heightened olfactory senses to find the two of them, and then she would inevitably kill them.

Even though she had killed many of his kind,

Guillermo had to try to subdue her, to break the queen's control over her. He couldn't abandon his friend, knew she was only a slave to mind-control.

Taking a gamble, Guillermo cocked his metal arm back and drove it up through the deck plate with all the force he could muster. The piece of corrugated metal flipped off of the floor and sent Dervish crashing into a nearby wall. She recovered quickly, and before he could fully climb out of the hole Dervish reached past him and grabbed Mitsuki. She yanked her out, throwing her into an ancient console that suddenly flickered to life.

"Dervish!" he screamed. "Fight the queen's control! I know you're in there somewhere!"

They were surrounded by five more bug soldiers, and all of them pointed their rifles at the two Terrans. Dervish gave off a scent and performed a quick wave of her hand that signaled for them to stand down before she moved in a blur to grab Mitsuki and slam her to the deck with a thud. Mitsuki cried out, reaching for Dervish's hand, but the Royal Guard was too quick, too strong, and Mitsuki wheezed heavily as the air was forced from her lungs by the blow.

"Leave her alone!" Guillermo roared, his voice a

loud growl. "Take it out on *me*!"

Dervish whirled around, her mandibles clicking together randomly. She froze for a moment, her claw-like hand reaching toward her eye as if in pain.

"That's it, Dervish," he shouted. "Fight it! Come back to me, old girl!"

Dervish's hand trembled, hovering above her large compound eye, but then she straightened, producing a small dagger from her belt and turning on Mitsuki.

He lowered his head and charged her, but she was ready for him, slicing his mending shoulder with the dagger as he struck her. She used his momentum to throw him toward the cockpit as two bug soldiers dove out of the way.

"The Queen has decided to end you, Terran," she said as she stalked forward, her head cocked to the side. "I am but her hand."

Guillermo lay with his back against the console, blue and red lights flickering and dancing, but his eyes looked past Dervish to Mitsuki who struggled to her feet. He looked at her and winked, and a little smile curled the edge of his mouth.

She shook her head, her eyes widening, her

mouth open in an expression of surprise.

He spun, his hands dancing over the controls, and then a static-laced voice sounded over the gunship's damaged comm system.

"Reactor overload in progress. All hands make preparations."

He used his metal fist to smash the controls and Dervish rushed forward, her knife driving deep into his side. The blade scraped a rib. He struck out blindly, hearing Dervish cough as his fist found her face, icky fluid splattering the far wall. She flailed in the air and fell to the deck and squirmed there. He used the momentum to stumble forward as the bug soldiers backed away from him again, following orders to a fault. He staggered to the hole in the deck, nearly fell in, and Mitsuki rushed forward, grabbing him under his arm, pulling the blade from his side.

A gout of blood spilled on the rusty metal floor.

"Pod," he uttered, and pointed to the far wall.

She heaved him over to the escape pod, a small one person pill shape that she hoped still worked, and he pulled her close to him as the door hissed shut. Through the glass they could see the bug soldiers opening fire on the pod, but the plasma bolts only left burn marks in the plasteel window as their pod fell out rather than shot out of the bottom of the gunship as per design. Three bug soldiers were expelled with it into the vacuum of the immense hangar bay.

"I can't feel my…" Guillermo stammered as he sat in the lone seat, Mitsuki on his lap. "I can't…"

And he tried to breathe, but his mouth coughed out a little glob of floating crimson.

"Just hold on," she said as a tear floated away from her eye and danced with the glob of blood.

The reactor failure, a peppering of explosive debris, shot them out of the hold like a bullet.

CHAPTER 42

"Good thing I'm small," said Mitsuki, her hand reaching past his neck to activate a life support buffer.

"Ok," he replied, his voice weak. "That should do it."

His breathing had become shallow, and there was a rattle that concerned her.

She was able to see out a small dirty porthole just to the left of Guillermo's shoulder, and in the light of Fraaz's single yellow star she could see the bug dreadnaught listing toward the planet, debris from the explosion littering behind it like a sparkling trail of stardust.

"I don't think they'll be following us anytime soon," she said, adjusting on his lap.

He only grunted, a half-hearted laugh that started as a wry smile and ended as a wince. She could smell the coppery scent of blood. The warmth of it was beginning to soak her clothes where she pressed against him in the cramped space, but she tried to keep her mind off of it and hope that he would get better like always.

He wasn't so sure.

"It's hard to breathe," he groaned. "You sure you hit the right switch on the life support?"

"Yes…well, I think so," she stammered. "I could have flushed the toilet for all I know."

He showed his crooked teeth for a moment, a film of blood on them, and then pursed his lips and hissed out a breath of air.

"Look around for a medkit. Surely this old bucket has one."

She placed her hands on his shoulders, her eyes wide.

"Guillermo, I don't think I could find it if I wanted to. We're kind of cramped here, probably falling toward the planet, and…"

"Just find it," he coughed. "What else have you got to do, anyway?"

That was all it took to break her resolve. She began to sob.

"You mean to tell me," he said, his voice quivering. "That the woman I saw take down a whiptail, who broke me out of their lair, is done? Get a grip!"

She stopped, then her brown eyes stared into his, and with some hesitation because of the grime leaned and kissed him, passionately, as if it were her last act. Her hand reached to the back of his head and pulled him close to her. He did the same, awkwardly, and gave in even though he could barely breathe. They needed this, fed off of it, and he determined that they would not die in this tiny floating tin can.

He pulled away from her gently, his hand on the nape of her neck, and his fingers brushed an odd bump just under her skin.

"What is that?" he whispered.

"A kiss," she said. "And now I'm regretting it."

"No. That bump on your neck."

She touched his hand, then past it to rub her skin and feel the little bump just beneath her hairline.

"I don't know," she said. "Is it important? Just where the bounty hunter stung me...said it was an inoculation."

Something slammed into the pod, a heavy metallic thump, and she shrieked in his ear. He ignored her, craning his neck to look out the porthole at the black dreadnaught which had somehow changed course and was floating listlessly in their direction. A slowly increasing orange glow from near the bottom of the pod told him another story.

They were descending toward Fraaz.

He looked at her, his face becoming pale, his lips a faint shade of blue.

"I don't think I know how to make this thing slow down," he said, his eyes glassy. "And I don't know if I'll make it with you. You have to promise me…"

"You'll make it!" she shouted, her voice very loud in the small space. "Shut up about dying, you crulling pig. I won't be alone!"

His eyes stared at her for a moment, no retort to her exclamation, and then his eyelids fluttered closed and he slumped against the wall. She pulled him up, using all the strength she had left to steady him as they fell toward the planet, followed fast by the broken dreadnaught. She wrapped her arms around his shoulders, squeezing him to her, then her hands explored his side. She could feel the blood oozing out of the wound left by Dervish, and she muttered a prayer to whomever was listening as the tears began to stream again.

The landing was much worse than she thought it would be.

The pod landed on the dark side of the planet. If it were not for the final few millijoules of energy left in the ancient power cells and the heavy padding within, their descent would have been abrupt and messy. Instead it was abrupt and jarring. The pod left a scar across the wasteland as it bounced and skidded to a final stop beside an ancient Terran structure, the walls eaten away by scavengers and vicious sandstorms common to the region.

The pod, a pill-shaped cocoon, spat the two of them out onto the sand without ceremony. The explosive hinges still capable of catapulting the door from the main housing sent it rocketing away like a rusty coin.

Mitsuki lay on top of a wheezing Guillermo, and she groaned as she rolled off onto the sand. She lay still for a moment in the darkness before stirring up what strength she had left to drag his limp body across the sand and into the shelter of the nearby structure. She propped up his head and shoulders, leaning him against a pockmarked wall, and then lay beside him to get some rest.

"Dervish," he rattled. "Dervish, I'm so sorry…"

All she could do was stare at the blanket of stars and watch as the remnants of the dreadnaught streaked across the sky like a meteor shower of orange and yellow. With one trembling hand she felt at the bump on her neck, not willing to tell him earlier how it was sore and itched terribly. She scratched at it, wondering whether the bump was an inoculation as she was told, but knowing now that it probably was something much more harmful.

She wanted to cut it out.

She looked around her for something sharp on a whim, but then her eyes began to droop and she snuggled in close to Guillermo to rest.

CHAPTER 43

She felt her arm being moved next, and her eyes flicked open to see Guillermo pulling at her hand. His mouth agape and his eyes two quivering orbs. He pointed to his side but was not making any noise, his lips a deep shade of blue.

Something far worse was happening to him now.

He writhed in the sand, his arms twisting up and down and his legs squirming, kicking the dust in a death dance of anguish. She stood immediately, her hands flying to the sides of her head as she frantically wondered what to do with him. She was not a surgeon, and he needed a surgeon.

He continued to use what little control he had to point at his side, and then he began to seize, his eyelids fluttering over the whites of his eyes, and she knelt next to him to examine the wound. It was purple all around, and had somehow closed up, but it was swelling horribly, as if something the size of her fist was embedded just under his bruised skin.

"O-open," he stammered, and she understood that the wound probably needed to be drained, but there was nothing sterile about her hands or anything else nearby.

As a final act before passing out, he grabbed her wrist with his robotic arm, and she felt like it would break as he pulled her close to him, close to the wound, and then let her go. She flexed her hand once, then held her breath as she placed two fingers on the wound, and the skin broke, oozing white pus. She pushed further, deeper, and a hiss of air and fluid escaped, spraying her leg with blood. Frantically she looked around for something to stop the bleeding, and out of the corner of her eye she saw the pod, its walls padded with a cloth that had been untouched for over a century.

Racing through the sand which made her short run feel like half a kilometer, she reached the pod and began desperately looking around for something to tear at the cloth. A chunk of loose paneling caught her eye and she pulled it free, nearly straining her back, and with a couple of stabs, her body adding momentum, she was able to punch a hole in the padding.

He groaned in the distance.

She tore a swath free and ran back to find Guillermo unconscious, his arms and legs splayed out and his grizzled chin against his chest. Quickly, she placed the wadded cloth against the wound and pressed hard, hearing a quivering grunt from Guillermo, and in moments he was breathing normally as whatever freakish healing ability he possessed went to work.

His breathing subsided, nearly stopped, and she leaned in close to listen to his chest. She tried to focus with the increasing sound of the wind whipping around the wall. The gale caused the structure somewhere far above them to creak. The wind picked up the sand around them, its abrasive grains slipping under clothing and into her mouth.

"Thank you," he whispered. "You're…"

She started at the sudden sound of his voice, then her smile lit up the darkness, and he returned the expression as best he could, his breathing still a gurgling wheeze.

She lay beside him then, mostly from exhaustion, and as the wind died down again the two of them slept through the night, at least until the heat of the morning light rising over the dunes forced them awake.

To her surprise, Guillermo was up and moving first, holding his side with his mechanical arm as he rummaged through the escape pod like some intergalactic vagrant. She approached him and he

turned to face her, his eyes bright and a smile on his lips
that somehow caused her stomach to flutter.

"You're up," he said, his voice low over the sound
of the wind. "I found some rations in here. Probably
not any good. But I also found a medkit that's pretty
much intact."

"Your wound," she said, one small hand touching
his side. "How did it…"

"Nanites," Guillermo offered, lifting his arm so
that she could examine the wound. "I was given a dose
of nanites by the docs back on the bug homeworld.
Along with this arm. I heal faster than normal, but it
looked like Dervish nicked me a little too deep.
Needed to relieve some pressure. Thanks for that."

"Dervish," she said.

He stopped moving for a moment, a dusty packet
of rations in one hand.

"I have hope that she can be saved," Guillermo
said finally. "She is being controlled by the queen, but I
saw something back there…something that gave me
hope that she can fight it. If she survived — and
knowing her, she probably did — I think we should still
try to help her break free. She might be the key to
stopping the queen, to resetting all of this."

"She tried to kill us."

"But didn't you see her hesitate? I know that the nanites might be working to break whatever control the queen has over her."

"You said nanites…I've never heard of such a thing," she said, reaching up and scratching at the bump on her neck. "But I guess you'll be fine, right?"

"The little buggers haven't let me down yet. Maybe they'll work for Dervish, too."

He paused, shook his head.

"Now, let's see what we can do about finding our way to another ship. This time maybe we won't get scooped up in orbit."

"So you're, like, invincible?" she asked. "I mean, how much is too much? Didn't seem to work to well for Dervish."

He reached into the pod and pulled out a small bag of tools.

"I think we saw the limit of mine last night," he said, handing her the bag. "It's probably having trouble with Dervish's physiology and they are having to work overtime. Could be that whatever is controlling her has neutralized most of them. I know that if I take too much damage, the nanites are not capable of working fast enough to heal me. I was told that the little bots were used by the Phaedran Empire ages ago, but they discontinued them for some reason. They seem to be better at repairing my stupid arm, but when it comes to flesh and bone—"

"Sure."

They spent the next few hours stripping the pod of all of its useful components, which were sparse. They managed to find a few bits of broken durasteel and wrapped them with some of the cloth from the padding to make crude knives, but mostly they needed food and the pod was useless in this regard. The food packs were covered with a gelatinous fungi.

They crested a few dunes before they could see in the distance something of a settlement, a small ring of buildings shredded and broken, their rusty metal frames visible as hash-marked protrusions that pointed at the pale blue sky. Cautiously they approached, their daggers ready, Guillermo still holding his side but moving more easily now as the nanites used precious resources to repair his damaged lung. This had an adverse effect on his complexion, and his pale skin made Mitsuki walk closer to him, her furtive glances turning into longer and longer stares.

He noticed.

They approached the settlement which they now could see was only a burned out fort long since abandoned by the Terrans who had nuked this planet. The light from Fraaz's star baked the ground around them as they crept into the shadow of an outlying structure. Mitsuki nudged Guillermo and pointed high into the rotted frame of a nearby edifice where three Fraaz hung upside down, their leathery wings wrapped around them like tobacco leaves around a cigar.

They appeared to be asleep.

Guillermo tapped Mitsuki on the shoulder and when she looked at him he pointed ahead of them where a large shuttle sat unattended. Her face shone through all the grime and sweat, and he couldn't help but huff out a slight whisper of a laugh before covering his mouth. Carefully, Mitsuki and Guillermo crept out across the sand, the wind from the east kicking up little dust devils that danced across the central square, and soon they reached the shuttle. Guillermo nearly punched the hull in frustration before he caught himself.

The shuttle was missing an engine.

CHAPTER 44

A few tense moments later, Guillermo and Mitsuki had snuck to the other side of the ring of burned out buildings where no Fraaz scavengers hung from the rafters. Dejectedly, Guillermo squatted next to a blackened duracrete wall and began to draw in the dust with a metallic finger.

"So what do we do now?" whispered Mitsuki, standing at the opposite wall, her arms folded.

"Nothing, I guess," he said aloud.

She grit her teeth and flashed wide eyes at him.

She peered around the wall at the square, at the old shuttle missing a key component, and then she squatted next to him.

He didn't acknowledge her, continuing to draw random designs in the dust.

"Could we search the outlying buildings?" she offered. "Maybe there's an engine or parts of one lying around."

He turned his head slowly and stared at her then, his face a blank mask. He at least stopped drawing for a bit. He let out a sigh, frowned, then stood up to pull at his blood-crusted shirt.

"If we search this place we'll have to deal with Moe, Larry and Curly over there," he said, jerking his thumb over his shoulder. "They won't take too kindly to a couple of Terrans going through their stash. If there *is* anything in their stash. I'll bet if we can find a stash of junk we'll find an engine…or parts we can use to make one."

"Moe, Larry…?"

"Never mind," he said. "I gotta get you some holovids to watch sometime."

She laughed softly.

"So how do we do this?" she whispered. "We don't have any weapons in case they attack us."

"So we work quietly," he said, and he peered discreetly around the wall at the clearing again. "The thing is, it'll take a lot of time to install an engine if we find one. That means fighting the stooges."

He looked again, and the three Fraaz, like three black drops of oil hung in the shadow of the ruined building on the far side of the clearing, swaying in the wind. Guillermo wondered if they were alive until he saw one of them twitch a wing. Guillermo motioned to Mitsuki and they began to move slowly around the outside of the ring of buildings, creeping through

charred holes in the wall and burned doorways.
Eventually they reached a pile of junk, a mound of
random items collected over time by the Fraaz
scavengers.

Guillermo glanced at the ceiling, then placed a
hand on Mitsuki.

Hanging near the rusty metal roof, little dots of
sunlight projected on its black fur, was a sleeping Fraaz
sentry.

"Didn't see Shemp," Guillermo whispered in
Mitsuki's ear. "I always liked Shemp."

She shrugged, then he pointed up to the ceiling
and she nodded, wide eyed.

In the pile of oily scrap, there was a large and
familiar rounded shape, something that could be an
engine or part of one but Guillermo wasn't sure, the
shadows cast across it obscuring his view. They crept
forward, and soon Guillermo placed a hand on the
rounded scrap of metal, and saw that it was indeed the
engine for the shuttle parked in the clearing. It was
sitting on a rubber wheeled cart with a strand of frayed
cable tied to it for towing. Annoyingly, the Fraaz had
piled several pieces of thin metal on top and around it
in order to cause the most noise if someone tried to

make off with it. They could clear the metal scraps, but it would take time, and there was too great a risk they would wake the stooges.

Guillermo and Mitsuki stared at each other, each taking a deep breath at the same time, and then a crack of thunder split the air in the distance, and the whine of engines grew louder and louder. Above them, the Fraaz sentry unfolded his wings and screeched, then fluttered toward the ground, landing with a graceless thud.

The Terrans bolted for the gaping hole in the wall where they had entered the room, but the Fraaz scurried toward them, baring his needle teeth and growling a wordless warning. Guillermo, following Mitsuki through the wall, paused to give the Fraaz a savage kick to the snout as he bounded out onto the hot sand. He stopped suddenly when he saw the slender shapes of two bug gunships zipping across the dunes toward them.

"Get inside!" he shouted, and he limped behind Mitsuki as she sprinted for one of the other buildings.

Once inside, they peered out a hole in the wall to see the stooges careering toward the landing bug craft, their harpoons bouncing harmlessly off of armored hulls. A figure emerged from the landing ramp of the closest ship, and in a few moments three of the stooges were downed by the rapid fire of orange bolts of light. The remaining stooge squawked and growled as he fluttered away like some horribly injured carrion bird.

The figure was not interested in the Fraaz anyway, and through the wobbly heat waves they watched it bound toward the settlement. Guillermo, now recognizing his old partner in the distance, grabbed Mitsuki by the arm and pulled her toward him, shouting a string of profanity.

"How the crull did she find us?" he screamed.

"I don't know," she replied. "But there has to be something in that scrap we can use to kill her."

He didn't answer, but ran toward the storage building, more of a gallop with his side still stabbing at him. She followed close behind, and in a few moments they were digging through the scraps of metal and twisted parts. Unfortunately, all they could manage were a few sharp pieces of durasteel. Mitsuki didn't quibble, grabbing a jagged shard and then standing just at the outside of the hole that faced the gunships. Guillermo could see Dervish coming, striding across the sand nimbly, her lesser weight a benefit to her movement.

Suddenly she stopped, and he wished he had a gun.

She raised her rifle, and Guillermo ran to tackle Mitsuki to the ground.

Three superheated bolts of carbon shot through the duracrete and embedded themselves in the opposite wall, one of them burrowing through the scrap metal. Guillermo and Mitsuki stared up at the new smoking hole in the wall just where Mitsuki had been standing moments ago.

Guillermo helped Mitsuki up and they ran for the opposite door, sprinting around the corner of the outside wall as two more bolts zipped past them. Guillermo had dealt with this gun before, but since the only defense was to run in a zig-zag pattern and keep a good distance, he knew they would tire before Dervish ran out of liquid carbon.

"Run that way!" he ordered Mitsuki, pointing at the shuttle sitting on the sand. "Don't follow me!"

Before she could respond, Guillermo ran back toward Dervish, ducking in and out of buildings as red hot carbon bolts cut through all obstacles like butter, eventually embedding in harder surfaces at the end of the gun's range. Dervish appeared between two buildings, her face still a mess from their last encounter. She leveled the gun at a charging Guillermo, shooting two bolts at him that zinged luckily past.

"Put that down and listen to me!" Guillermo screamed, charging forward.

She did, dropping the gun to the sand and extending her electroglaive, the blade rippling with blue energy. She struck at him when he came close, and blocked the pommel end with his metallic arm, a loud clang resounding in the small courtyard. He countered with a kick to Dervish's midsection, and she easily dodged it, countering with the pommel end of her own weapon, catching Guillermo under the chin.

He fell back, arms and legs sprawling, and she twirled the electroglaive around above her head before bringing it down on him again. He parried it at the last second with his unnaturally fast robotic arm. He tried the kick again, this time using the leverage afforded by his supine position, and connected with her lower thorax, causing her to squeal out a vibrato of angry pain. He slid his arm down the electroglaive to grasp it firmly and twist, bending it to almost a ninety degree angle. She squealed again and kicked him, this time striking the knife wound, and the crack he heard was drowned out by the flash of blinding pain that accompanied it.

He stood, nearly swooned, holding his side. Dervish approached him slowly and he had to try to reach her somehow.

"Dervish! Crull it all!" he shouted. "What about your oath? What about our bond?"

She stopped, her head twitching to the side again, her quivering hand reaching for one compound eye, but then a chunk of duracrete struck her from behind. Mitsuki was charging forward, striking the Royal Guard at full speed, knocking her to the sand. Guillermo nearly swooned, his wound bleeding again, a side effect of the toe claws on Dervish's feet. A gush of red blood colored the white sand.

Dervish bounded to her feet and pulled a long knife from her belt, and now the two females circled each other, each armed with a blade. Dervish moved first, and before Guillermo could stop it, the Royal Guard's blade nicked Mitsuki just under her left eye. Mitsuki used the momentum of Dervish's strike to grasp at her arm, jabbing the shard of durasteel forward, but it scraped harmlessly off of Dervish's exoskeleton.

"No!" Guillermo shouted. "I was getting through to her!"

Dervish jerked away then, spinning forward to drive the knife toward Mitsuki's face, but she ducked, coming up under the bug with both hands firmly grasping the shard, severing a tendon in her attacker's arm. Without a scream, without a sound at all save shuffling sand, Dervish responded by swinging around and kicking Mitsuki with one clawed foot, sending her sprawling across the ground.

The carbon-rod gun was just at Dervish's feet, and she quickly grabbed it with her uninjured arm, spun, and shot at Mitsuki.

The bolt narrowly missed as Mitsuki rolled to the left, and then ran. Guillermo stumbled forward, his side oozing blood, and dove at Dervish, his mechanical arm grabbing the gun and forcing the barrel to the ground. He pounded at it, damaging the housing only, and with his other arm he held on to Dervish. The effect was more like a small child trying to prevent his mother from leaving for work. She brushed him aside, kicking him to the ground again. Guillermo saw Mitsuki dash into a nearby structure before he rolled to his right and placed a hand over his wound.

Dervish stood over him, her injured arm hanging limp at her side, and she began to click and vibrate the five sets of mandibles, fluid dripping from her chin.

"I will kill your mate, Terran," came the voice of the queen. "And then I will leave you here to die on this dead world."

Guillermo couldn't give up on her.

"Dervish!" he shouted, his voice cracking. "Dervish you have to fight her control. Remember your oath to the real Queen. There are nanites flowing through you, too…because of me. My gift. Now fight it!"

He watched her closely then, and a mandible on the bottom of her jaw twitched, then she shook her head so fast it blurred.

"I," she chittered. "I serve the Queen. Her will…is my own."

She turned then, and Guillermo fought through the pain and stood, watching her walk away from him, his body too exhausted to act. She raised her wrist to her jagged mouth and a holographic image appeared.

"Destroy this settlement…kill the Terrans…," she clicked. "Then extract me."

In the distance, barely visible between two ruined buildings, the gunships began to lift from the sand and fly toward their position. He fell to the sand as the massive guns hanging from their undercarriages began to glow and then fire bright yellow bolts at the very building in which Mitsuki had taken shelter. He screamed, gathering every ounce of strength to run toward where he had seen Mitsuki hide, but the gunships circled the settlement, blasting the ruined buildings to fiery blooms of debris that scattered into the clearing and pinged off the hull of the shuttle.

As he stumbled under the bulky shuttle to protect himself from the shrapnel, caught a glimpse of Mitsuki running from one of the buildings just as it crumbled to the ground. He called out to her, but she didn't hear him, and before he could say anything else Dervish was trotting across the sand toward her, knife in hand. He stood to his feet and screamed as Dervish reached her. He ran toward them, but the Royal Guard, the person who had saved his life many times, sliced Mitsuki across the back with her blade. Dervish stopped, watched her fall, then looked back at Guillermo before disappearing on the other side of the rubble.

Rage exploded out of Guillermo as he glared

across the sand at the motionless body of Mitsuki. His scream, nearly inaudible over the roar of flames, humming gunships and crumbling structures, was all that Guillermo could hear.

He watched helplessly as Dervish boarded one of the gunships via the landing ramp and then ascended into the bleak sky.

His body protested, but he ran forward, kneeling in the dust next to Mitsuki, and the other gunship landed nearby to deposit five bug soldiers on the sand. He turned to face them, his eyes two red orbs of tears, and with gnashing teeth ran at one of them. His metal fist connected with the bug's head and obliterated it instantly, and as the others raised their rifles to fire at him he was already on the second one, ripping the soldier's arm from his body like plucking the wings off a fly. The others retaliated, firing at Guillermo with their plasma guns, but the bolts were deflected by a mysterious bubble of force that appeared around him as he approached them, his eyes wild with hatred.

If the other three bug soldiers could scream they would have.

Afterward, he shook all over, his shoulders rising and falling, his teeth bared. He screamed something unintelligible, a primal roar that echoed off of the rubble around him. With care he gathered Mitsuki's limp body in his arms, and with newfound strength, ran to the bug's abandoned gunship.

CHAPTER 45

A warp orb appeared at the edge of an ionic storm, a glittering purple barrier at the edge of the Fraaz system, a place that swallowed the remnants of the Phaedran empire after the rebellion had ended. A bug gunship emerged, its engines cooling down from the gravitic anomaly it created to travel through warp space. It floated forward on maneuvering thrusters as Dervish and her three soldier crew prepared their craft to signal the queen's armada.

The Terrans were finally eradicated.

Dervish sat upon a spartan command chair, her claw-like fingers tapping at a console made from a chitinous material, and suddenly she could hear the voice of the Queen in her mind.

<You have done well, my guard.> came the message, not really in words but in impressions and chemical coded sensations. *<Enjoy the rest and pleasure of my favor.>*

A chemical flood washed her brain then, a cool sensation of her pleasure centers reacting to the Queen's telepathic command, allowed by the C'Tuul'U'Hindra, the ancient control device the queen wore upon her brow.

<Wait for me there, my servant.> warbled the soft sensations of the queen's communique. *<I will send a dreadnaught to retrieve you. The Five Rims will soon be once again our people's empire.>*

Dervish rested, basking in the soft chemical glow of her queen's pleasure, but something within her tried to fight it, tried to struggle against the arachnid things inside her brain that forced her to do the will of her queen, and a fluttering hand reached for one eye. Now and again she would experience glimpses of what she was before, of her time with the Terran, but it would be washed away by the chemical flood.

She lay her head back and rested, feeling the gratifying sensation of her reward.

Something violently rocked her out of her seat and sent her tumbling to the deck. She rose, and through the view port ahead of her she saw the unmistakable shape of a bug gunship sail by, debris from her own ship floating fast after it.

They had rammed her.

"You like that, Dervish?" said the Guillermo's floating holographic head appearing on her comm panel. She read his lips as they snarled at her. "You took Mitsuki from me, so I'm coming for you!"

Plasma blasts rocked the hull of her gunship before she could reach the shield control, and a new volley immediately lit up the space around her ship as those shields engaged. Silently, she took her seat again and her crew ran to operate the guns. Something within her itched and scratched, something trying to stop her from defending her ship.

I have betrayed my friend and deserve his wrath.

She blocked it out.

She would not fail her queen.

The gunship blasted toward them again, and this time it hit them nose to nose, the shields buckling, and the hull screamed in protest. She fired up the overheated engines and pushed the throttle forward, dropping the ship beneath Guillermo's pirated gunship. Her crew opened fire on his undercarriage and she found that he had not engaged his shields at all, as chunks of his gunship exploded outward toward her.

His ship listed to the side, but then her ship was rocked by something else. The indicator light blinked, signifying a tractor beam had locked on to her. He was pulling her toward him, or rather pulling himself toward her. She cut in the maneuvering thrusters to aid with her overtaxed engines, but it was too late. Soon she could feel the familiar vibration in the hull of docking clamps locking into position.

He was coming aboard.

It would be personal.

I deserve his wrath.

She leaped from her seat, landing on the deck and sprinting to the airlock just as he used his metallic fist to punch a hole through the plasteel porthole on the inner door. The room suddenly equalized, and she could feel the air squeezing on her exoskeleton. He reached through, pulling the latch and kicking the door open to rush onto her ship and lunge at her. His face was contorted in a horrific mask as he swung at her with his robotic fist and she countered with a kick to his abdomen. He wheezed out air, scrambled forward, and then he had her by the arm.

She felt the excruciating fire of pain that was his metallic grip as it crushed her exoskeleton and threatened to rip her injured arm from the shoulder joint. She fell backward, wrapping her powerful legs around his neck and squeezing, but this only seemed to anger him more.

"Please, Guillermo…please…" she tried to say, but her mouth was too damaged to mimic his language.

Alarms flashed brilliant colors on every wall and ceiling of the ship as she could feel the hull begin to groan. As she struggled, her bug crew informed her that they were being drawn toward the ionic cloud...by something unknown. She called for them to help her fight the Terran, and they suddenly appeared in the room with her. Guillermo broke free of her then, becoming a blur, rending the crew into a pile of limbs and body parts in seconds. Their fluids soon dripped from the walls and ceiling in a horrific display.

Guillermo had somehow changed. What little injuries her crew could inflict on the Terran healed before her eyes, and his strength was incredible.

His eyes were glowing red.

She shrank back, rushing to the console to do something, anything, to keep them from falling into the ionic cloud, but it was too late. Bolts of energy began to dance across consoles as they fell deeper in, and suddenly she felt something inside her head like hot coals searing through her brain. She fell to the deck, and her own fluids dribbled down her face as tiny white arachnids slipped past her compound eye and screeched and squealed in their final death throes. Free from the control of the queen, she turned her head and stared above her, her mouth trying desperately to form Terran words, but the injuries were too extensive.

Guillermo stood over her, his chest heaving, and then she drifted away into the dark.

CHAPTER 46

Guillermo had collapsed.

He lay on the deck of Dervish's gunship, surrounded by the remnants of her crew, his body sprayed with the fluids these bugs called blood. Mitsuki had been killed, but he didn't remember much after that. As he struggled to sit up his eyes opened to the darkness now enveloping both gunships, the only light produced by strobing warning lights.

The ionic cloud had sapped all power except for emergency batteries.

He finally stood to his feet, using his arm to brace himself against a command chair. In the faint strobe of the warning lights, consoles around him were smoking, and he looked to the deck to see Dervish, her body broken and damaged. He was suddenly blind-sided with the memory of what he did.

He knelt beside her, taking her slender hand in his own and touching the two fingers gently, but she did not respond. He stood, but then felt a pain throughout his body that caused him to crouch on the deck next to her. A flaming ache shot through his muscles, seeming to emanate from his bones, and he slumped against the

base of the command chair and began to convulse, a
sound rolling out of his lungs like he was being
squeezed by a giant hand.

Dervish suddenly turned her head, her mandibles
clicking out broken Terran speech.

"G—Guiller—," she stammered. "So—so sorry.
Forg— Forgive…"

Her head lolled a bit, then she caught herself. He
managed to fight past the darkness closing in on his
vision, reaching for her hand again. She lightly grasped
it, just as his eyes began to fill with heavy tears.

"What have I done?" he slurred. "I don't
understand…so sorry…"

"You— You had eve— every right…"

"No," he said, moving close to her now, his face
directly above hers.

She coughed out a gout of fluid.

"No," he repeated. "I…something came over me…
the rage was too strong to control. What did I do?"

She did not answer him, her head rolling to the side,
her mandibles going slack. He shook her, but she
didn't respond. After a moment he sat back against the
control chair pedestal and began to sob. He closed his
eyes, the tears wetting his face as his moans echoed

within the cramped command deck. He nearly ignored the faint hiss of air escaping somewhere from a bulkhead.

There was a popping sound and the faint hiss suddenly became a roar.

He staggered to his feet, swooning once and catching himself on the command chair, and then he stomped toward the airlock to board the other gunship. Within he found Mitsuki's body lying on the deck, discarded there after he had brought them to this place beyond the ionic cloud.

He stared at Mitsuki in silence, time no longer real.

He cleared his head, ran his fingers through his hair, then toggled the airlock door only to find that it would not respond. Nothing would respond. The two gunships, locked together in a death embrace, had been drained of all power.

He sat in the command chair of his own ship then, staring at the plasteel window in front of him, and he could see in the distance a star, a bright yellow star. The ionic cloud danced in the distance, a purple ribbon that had not killed them.

Yet.

He heard another strange popping sound, and then

the gravity generator quit. Mitsuki floated from the deck, her arms spreading out from her as if to embrace him, and he pushed away from his chair, catching her in his arms. He held her then, the two of them in a cold embrace, and he reached up and cradled her head against his shoulder, closed his eyes, and waited for oblivion.

EPILOGUE

The twin bug gunships were swallowed up by an immense shadow that slowly moved across their wrecked hulls, floating serenely in the ocean of space beyond the ionic cloud.

"Two life signs," said a deep voice. "One erratic, the other extremely faint...and something else. I need to get them in the hold for further scans."

"Are they from the Five Rims?" said another, a female voice, hard, as if it belonged to someone accustomed to war.

"Negative," said the other. "Terran."

An emerald beam shot from an emitter on the hull of a massive black ship, an immense craft, its bulk blotting out the light from the nearby star. Its surface was decorated with metallic reliefs of Terran skulls, each one with gaping jaws set in a perpetual scream. The gunships were drawn toward it by the beam, the soft light enveloping them and protecting them from the vacuum of space.

Swallowed by a hold, the doors slowly closing, the ships came to rest within an atmospheric bubble.

"Prepare medical crews," said the woman. "They

are home at last."

Roger Colby is an English teacher by trade, making the lives of teens in his class difficult yet rewarding even if they cannot see the use for the important skills he is teaching them (for the most part). He is a father of four rambunctious children and is husband to a wonderful, beautiful, understanding wife who gives him space to write about weird places and even weirder happenstances. He has many dogs, cats, and chickens.

It is a noisy house.

Other novels by Roger Colby:

The Transgression Box, 2009
This Broken Earth, 2012
Come Apart, 2014
The Terminarch Plot, 2015

All are available on Amazon.com.

Guillermo's adventures are not over. They will continue in the forthcoming novel *The Shibboleth Code* in 2017.

Roger is also writing a Lovecraftian satire adventure novel about the current political climate in Oklahoma. Look for it in October 2016!

If you liked this novel (or if you didn't) please write a review. It would be much appreciated. Thank you for reading!

www.ingramcontent.com/pod-product-compliance
Lightning Source LLC
Chambersburg PA
CBHW062013170626
46813CB00001B/137